ERLE STANLEY GARDNER

- Cited by the *Guinness Book of World Records* as the #1 bestselling writer of all time!

- Author of more than 150 clever, authentic, and sophisticated mystery novels!

- Creator of the amazing Perry Mason, the savvy Della Street, and dynamite detective Paul Drake!

- THE ONLY AUTHOR WHO OUTSELLS AGATHA CHRISTIE, HAROLD ROBBINS, BARBARA CARTLAND, AND LOUIS L'AMOUR *COMBINED*!

Why?
Because he writes the best, most fascinating whodunits of all!

You'll want to read every one of them,
from
BALLANTINE BOOKS

Also by Erle Stanley Gardner
Published by Ballantine Books:

The Case of the
Toubled Trustee

Erle Stanley Gardner

BALLANTINE BOOKS • NEW YORK

Foreword

Whenever people who are familiar with the outstanding figures in the field of legal medicine get together for informal shoptalk, the name of Dr. Leopold Breitenecker, of Vienna, will probably be mentioned.

My close friend, Dr. LeMoyne Snyder, who is both an attorney at law and an M.D., who has specialized in the field of forensic medicine and whose book, *Homicide Investigation* is one of the most authoritative books on the subject, spent quite a bit of time working and studying with Dr. Breitenecker in Vienna. He has told me much about the man's ability.

Too few people appreciate the importance of legal medicine and very few people appreciate the ramifications of the subject.

The average individual thinks of legal medicine in terms of the investigation of murders; legal medicine not only covers a wide scope but the field is constantly being enlarged.

The expert in legal medicine is being called upon daily to answer questions upon which important issues depend.

A man is smoking in bed. The house burns and the body is charred beyond recognition: Did the man have a heart attack, drop a cigarette and so cause the fire; or was he intoxicated when he met his death through suffocation or from the flames?

The medicolegal expert can give the answers, and where there is a certain type of insurance the answer may be important.

A body is found in bed: Was the body moved from some other place after death and placed in the bed?

The medicolegal expert can usually answer that question.

Were injuries inflicted before death or after death? What was the direction of the bullet wound? Which is the wound of entrance and which the wound of exit? How far was the gun from the body when it was discharged? Was the death murder or suicide?

Many, many times in cases where medicolegal experts were not called in, these questions have been answered erroneously. But the expert in the field of forensic medicine not only gives answers to these questions, he is able to demonstrate that his answers are correct. The international recognition of Dr. Breitenecker was expressed when he was sent by U Thant (UNO) into the Congo in 1962 to clarify the circumstances of the death of three members of the International Red Cross, and again, in 1964, when U Thant called him in to investigate the murder of an English officer in the Cypriot conflict.

And, since he is one of the world's outstanding experts in this important field,

I dedicate this book to my friend,

LEOPOLD BREITENECKER, M.D.
Professor and present Dean of the Faculty
of Medicine, University of Vienna.

ERLE STANLEY GARDNER

Chapter 1

Perry Mason, entering his office, grinned at Della Street and said, "What's in the mail, Della, anything startling?"

She indicated the pile of letters on Mason's desk. "The usual, people who want."

"Want what?"

"People who want you to make talks; write letters of endorsement, donate some intimate article for a celebrity auction."

"What else is new?" Mason asked.

Della Street rolled her eyes in an exaggerated pantomime of passionate interest.

"If," she said, "you want any efficiency whatever out of Gertie, your romantic receptionist, you had better get Kerry Dutton out of the office."

"And who is Kerry Dutton?" Mason asked.

"He is a youngish gentleman whose clothes are quietly elegant. He has a cameo-like profile, brown, wavy hair, steel-gray eyes, a very nice mouth; probably a thirty-six chest and a thirty waist. He is driving Gertie half crazy. She can't take her eyes off him."

"What does he want?" Mason asked.

"That," she said, "is the mystery. The man's card says that he is an investment counselor. He wants to see you about a matter that is very personal and exceedingly urgent."

Mason said, "I don't want to make any investments. I don't—"

"A professional matter," she interrupted.

Mason said, "My specialty is murder cases and trial work. What the devil would I want with an investment counselor?"

"I intimated as much," Della Street said.

"He wouldn't tell you what it was all about?"

"No, only that it was a highly personal matter involving something which must be handled in complete confidence and with the greatest of tact."

Mason said, "I'll take a look at him, at any rate that will get him away from Gertie's romantic gaze.

"How old is he, Della?"

"I would say thirty-one or thirty-two."

"And," Mason said, "I suppose his shoes are polished, his nails well manicured, his tie faultless, his appearance impeccable."

"Isn't all that supposed to go with an investment counselor?" Della Street asked.

Mason suddenly became thoughtful. "Hang it," he said, "I may have been doing the guy an injustice. Show him in, Della, and we'll find out what he wants."

Della Street nodded, left the office, and a few moments later returned, leading Kerry Dutton into the office.

"Mr. Dutton, Mr. Mason," she said.

Mason met the unflinching gray eyes, gave the man a brief appraisal from head to foot, then got up to shake hands. "How are you, Mr. Dutton?" he said.

"This is a great honor," Dutton said. "I am sorry I had to come without an appointment, Mr. Mason, but the matter is one of extreme urgency."

"Tell me generally what it's about," Mason invited. "I take it you're consulting me professionally?"

"Yes, indeed."

"My work," Mason said, "is largely in other fields. I doubt that I can help you. You're probably wasting time for both of us."

"You defend criminals, don't you?" Dutton asked.

"Yes."

"That's what I want you for."

"Who's the criminal?" Mason asked.

Dutton touched his breast with his left forefinger.

Mason studied his visitor with eyes that were steady and penetrating.

2

"You've been arrested and are out on bail?" he asked.

Dutton shook his head. "I haven't been arrested. That's why I came to you. I would like to keep from being arrested."

"You have perhaps embezzled money?"

"Yes."

"From whom?"

"From the account of one Desere Ellis."

"How much have you embezzled?"

"Looking at it one way it's a quarter of a million dollars."

Mason shook his head. "Every man," he said, "is entitled to his day in court. Every man is entitled to a lawyer to represent him, but a lawyer is not a partner in crime. From the facts as you tell them, you not only cannot escape arrest but, if I were to represent you, I would pick up that telephone and call the police."

"Wait a minute. You don't know the facts."

"I know enough of them from your own admissions."

"May I tell the story my way?"

Mason looked at his wrist watch. "I'll give you two minutes," he said, "but I'm busy. Your case doesn't appeal to me and your type doesn't appeal to me."

Dutton flushed.

Mason gave him no invitation to sit down, and Dutton remained standing.

"Templeton Ellis, the father of Desere Ellis, was one of my clients," he said. "He died four years ago. At the time of her father's death, Desere was twenty-three and was mixed up with a lot of people of whom her father didn't approve.

"He left a will containing a spendthrift trust. I was the trustee. Desere was to have the income as I saw fit to give it to her for her needs. She could have as much of the principal as I felt was advisable. I was given sole discretion in handling the funds; the right to invest and reinvest. I was to serve without bond."

"I see," Mason said. "He left you with absolute power."

"Yes. He did that to protect his daughter from herself."

3

"And what did he do," Mason asked pointedly, "to protect his daughter from you?"

"Nothing," Dutton said.

Mason's silence was eloquent.

"Now then," Dutton went on, "the amount of money that he left was around one hundred thousand dollars. In the four years since his death, I have given his daughter approximately a hundred and ten thousand dollars."

Mason frowned. "I thought you said you embezzled a quarter of a million."

"In a way, I have."

"I don't understand."

"Desere's father wanted me to keep intact the securities he had left, but I had the *power* to buy and sell.

"All right. I bought and I sold.

"One of her father's favorite stocks was a dog, the Steer Ridge Oil and Refining Company. I sold that stock without letting anyone know I had done so. I sold some of the other no-goods in the portfolio, stocks the father had held onto more for sentimental reasons than for sound business reasons." Dutton said. "I divided the money I received into three approximately equal amounts. One third I invested in blue-chip securities; the other I invested in securities which I felt had a strong opportunity for gain; and the remaining third, I used in real estate speculation in communities where I felt there would be development. I turned these properties over at a profit, put them in my own name, pyramided profits, and have netted a quarter of a million dollars."

"What about taxes?" Mason asked.

"I had the profit-making properties in my own name. I paid the capital gains taxes from the profits."

"What about annual accountings?"

"I have never made one, and the beneficiary has never asked for one."

"Hasn't she wanted to know what was happening to her money?"

"She thinks she knows. She thinks she has just about exhausted all the trust funds. I have given her more than two thousand dollars a month for all the period the trust has been in effect."

"Has she saved any of that?" Mason asked.

"Saved any? Heavens, no! She's spent that and probably has a few IOUs out. She is a pushover for all sorts of worthy and unworthy causes."

Mason caught Della Street's eye. "I see," he said.

Dutton watched him anxiously. "I hope you do," he said.

Mason studied his visitor for a moment, then said, "You have been guilty of all sorts of legal violations. You have mingled trust funds with your own; you have embezzled property; you have defrauded your client and betrayed your trust."

"Exactly," Dutton said. "I felt, however, that it was the thing to do."

"And what do you want me to do about all this?" Mason asked.

Dutton said, "Within three months, the trust will terminate. I have to make an accounting at that time and turn over all the trust monies to Desere."

"And I take it," Mason said, "you're not going to be able to make restitution."

"Restitution?" Dutton said in surprise. "Why, I have the entire fund intact. I have simply kept the properties in my name."

Mason regarded him thoughtfully. "Sit down," he suddenly invited.

"Thank you," Dutton said, and took a seat.

"Suppose you tell me," Mason said, "exactly what was the idea."

Dutton said, "I tried to do my best to protect Desere's interests. One hundred thousand dollars is not a great deal of money if you look at it in one way; in another way, it is a very great deal of money.

"At the time of her father's death, the people with whom Desere was running around had long hair, wore beards, had dirty fingernails, were left-wing idealists, and looked down on her as an heiress. They dipped into her money right and left, patronized her and considered her a square. She went

5

overboard trying to live up to their ideals so they'd respect her. They took her money but always looked on her as an outsider. She's a sensitive young woman who was hurt, lonely, and eager to be accepted as one of the crowd.

"Her father thought four years would give her a more mature perspective."

"And it was to protect her from that type of associate that her father made his spendthrift trust?"

"Yes. He wanted to protect her from herself. Undoubtedly her father's idea was that I would clamp down on the money she was to receive; that I would bring financial pressure to bear to force her to drop her friends and form her friendships from another environment. In fact, he intimated as much to me before his death."

"Why didn't you do it?" Mason asked.

"Because that would have been the wrong way to play my cards," Dutton said. "I realized that if she represented a large sum of money to these individuals, an attempt would be made to exploit her simply to secure a financial advantage. I wanted her friends to believe the trust fund would be exhausted.

"If, on the other hand, I could build up enough speculative profits which she knew nothing about so that I could afford to dish out her money to her with a liberal hand, she would spend it and any prospective fortune hunter would then regard her as a woman who had gone through her inheritance and, as such, she would be ostracized from the beatnik crowd."

"And you risked going to jail for this?" Mason asked.

"I want you to keep me from going to jail," Dutton said. "While I had taken chances on mingling the trust funds with my own assets, I had always held them in my name as trustee without disclosing the beneficiary of the trust."

"Suppose you had died?" Mason asked.

"I am in good health. I have no intention of dying in the near future."

Mason said, "Every week several hundred persons are slaughtered on the highways in a red harvest. None of these people had any intention of dying when they started out."

Dutton grinned. "I am one of those who *didn't* get killed on a weekend."

Mason looked at Dutton and said, "You're a young man."

"It depends on what you consider young. I consider myself quite mature. I'm thirty-two."

"And Desere?"

"She'll be twenty-seven in a few months."

"When you started handling this trust you were still in your late twenties?"

Dutton flushed and said, "That's right."

"Do you," Mason asked suddenly, "love her that much?"

"What!" Dutton exclaimed, snapping back in the chair and sitting very straight.

Mason said, "You have your career ahead of you. Apparently, you have a remarkable aptitude in your chosen profession. In order to protect Desere Ellis and keep her from being the victim of fortune hunters, you have jeopardized your entire professional career and apparently haven't gained a thing by it.

"Now you are talking to a lawyer. Lawyers are not noted for being particularly naïve, so perhaps you had better tell me the *real* story."

Dutton sighed, looked for an embarrassed moment at Della Street, then blurted out, "All right, I love her. I have always loved her, and I don't want her to know it the way things are now."

"Why?"

"Because she would never think of me in that way. Her attitude toward me is one she would show to a much older man. . . . Well, I'm sort of a big brother; a species of uncle. I don't talk her language. I don't mingle with the set that appeals to her. At the present time, she regards me only as the custodian of her money. Her set regards me as 'square.' "

"Were you so successful four years ago," Mason asked, "that Desere's father thought his daughter's financial affairs would be better in your hands than in those of some more experienced and older banker?"

Dutton hesitated.

"Go on," Mason said.

"All right," Dutton told him, "her father wanted to— Well, he liked me. He thought I might have a steadying influence on Desere— She was running with that crazy crowd. She went overboard for a lot of fads and fancies."

"And her father hoped that if she had to see a lot of you in connection with money matters she'd fall in love with you?"

"I guess that was partly his idea. He wanted to protect her from herself, and he may have had some idea of having her fall in love with me. He knew how I felt toward her.

"Actually, like so many schemes which fail to take human nature into consideration, the thing worked out just the opposite. She thinks of me as a moneygrubber. Our difference in ages has been accentuated."

"And you've been in love with her for four years?"

"Five."

"And never told her how you felt?"

"Of course I did. That was more than four years ago."

"What did she say?"

"She felt sorry for me. She said it was simply that I'd built up a synthetic feeling for her. She said she'd be a younger sister to me if I'd take her on that basis; that if I was going to persist in this crazy idea of being in love with her it would mean she couldn't see me any more. It would spoil the friendship."

"So you took it on that basis?" Mason asked.

"I've been waiting," Dutton said.

"Did her father have any idea he was dying?"

"Yes. He knew. The doctors gave him eight months. They were too optimistic. He lasted six."

"And now you feel that the will and the spendthrift trust didn't work out the way he had anticipated?"

Dutton said, "It had exactly the opposite effect. For a few months, Desere was so terribly hurt and angry that she would hardly speak to me.

"She felt that her father had repudiated her; that he had insulted her intelligence; that he was trying to dominate her life even after he had passed away and— Well, she's like a wild colt. She doesn't want any restrictions. Show her a fence and she tries to jump it. Come toward her with a halter and she wants to run; and if she gets cornered, she wants to bite and kick.

"After the will was read, she felt her father had crowded her into a corner, so she started biting and kicking."

"And, I take it," Mason said, "you were the target?"

"That's right."

"And you felt that embezzling the trust assets would make everything all right?"

"I wasn't trying to make things all right. I was trying to keep them from going all wrong."

"How?"

"She'd be a target for dead-beat fortune hunters if they knew the truth. Even as it is, she has a beatnik no-good moving in on her. He wants to marry her and 'manage' the few thousand she's going to get on the termination of the trust."

Mason smiled. "You don't approve of him as a husband for Desere?"

Dutton said grimly, "If he marries her, I'll—I don't know *what* I would do, but *someone* should shoot the guy."

Mason regarded Dutton thoughtfully. "Perhaps," he suggested, "you should be a little more aggressive in your romantic affairs."

"I have to play the waiting game a little longer," Dutton said.

"You've been playing it without any results for four years now," Mason said.

"Five," Dutton corrected. "I felt that as Desere grew more mature the difference in our ages would become insignificant. I want her to stop thinking of me as an older brother—a much older brother."

Mason said, "All right, I'm glad you've come clean. Now, I want you to do three things. First, make me a check for a thousand dollars as a retainer. Second, sign the undated declaration of trust, listing all the securities that are in your name but which you are holding as trustee for Desere

Ellis. You don't necessarily need to tell her about it, but get a record that these properties are being held only as a trustee under the will, then if you die she is protected."

"Third?" Dutton asked.

"Try to get Miss Ellis to come in to see me," Mason said. "I want to talk with her."

"Why?"

"Someone has to tell her that there is more money coming to her at the termination of the trust than she had anticipated, and someone has to tell her why. If you try to tell her, you have to sketch yourself as a heel. If I tell her, I *may* be able to put you in the position of a hero."

"Look here," Dutton said, "you can't tell her how I feel toward her. You can't—"

"Don't be foolish," Mason interrupted. "I'm not running a matrimonial agency; I'm running a law office. You're going to pay me to keep you out of trouble. I want to keep you out of trouble.

"Your love life is none of my business except as it affects the job I have to do."

Dutton took a checkbook from his pocket and started writing a check.

Chapter 2

Mason entered his private office the next morning to find Della Street opening the morning mail. He stood for a few moments watching her with appreciative eyes.

"Thanks," he said abruptly.

She looked up in surprise. "For what?"

"For just being," Mason said. "For being so much a part of things, so completely efficient and . . . and all the rest of it."

"Thank *you*," she said, her eyes suddenly soft.

"Any progress?"

"On what?" she asked.

"Come, come," Mason said, smiling. "Don't try to pull the wool over *my* eyes. On the romance, of course."

"The Dutton case?"

"Exactly."

"Nothing so far," she said. "Give the man a little time."

"He may not have as much time as he thinks," Mason said, seating himself in the client's overstuffed chair and watching Della Street's smoothly graceful figure as she stood at the desk opening letters, putting them in three piles—the urgent on the left-hand corner of the desk, the personal-answer-required in the middle, and the general run-of-the-mill for secretarial attention on the right.

"Want some advice?" she asked.

Mason grinned. "That's why I brought the subject up."

She said, "You can't play Dan Cupid."

"Why not?"

"You don't have the build. You wear too many clothes, and you lack a bow and arrow."

Mason grinned. "Keep talking."

"Sometimes," Della Street said, choosing her words carefully as though she had rehearsed them, "a woman will be close to a man for a long time, seeing him in the part in which he has cast himself and, unless he makes some direct approach, not regarding him as a romantic possibility."

"And under those circumstances?" Mason asked.

"Under those circumstances," Della Street said, "nature gave the male the prerogative of taking the initiative; and if he isn't man enough to take it, it is quite possible the girl will *never* see him as a romantic possibility."

"Go on," Mason told her.

"But the one thing that would definitely wreck everything would be for someone else to try and take the initiative on behalf of this individual."

"Longfellow, I believe, commented on that in the poem dealing with John Alden and Priscilla," Mason said.

Della Street nodded.

"All right," Mason told her, "I've been forewarned. You want me to keep my bungling masculine touch under cover, is that it?"

The phone on Della Street's desk rang.

She flashed him a quick smile, picked up the receiver and said, "Yes, Gertie," to the receptionist.

She said, "Wait a moment. Hold on, Gertie, I'll see."

Della Street turned to Perry Mason. "Desere Ellis is in the office," she said.

Mason grinned. "Let's take a look, Della."

"Just a moment," Della Street said. "She is accompanied by a Mr. and Mrs. Hedley, apparently a mother and son."

"They are all three of them together?" Mason asked.

Della Street nodded. "As Gertie whispered confidentially, the mother is a determined creature with a rattrap mouth and monkey eyes; and the son is pure beatnik with a beard and a cool-cat manner which makes her flesh crawl. You know how Gertie is and how she loves to make snap appraisals of clients."

"And generally she's right," Mason said. "Have Gertie send the three of them in."

Della Street relayed the message, then went to the door communicating with the outer office and held it open.

Hedley came in first—a broad-shouldered young man with a spade beard, calmly contemptuous eyes, a sport shirt open at the neck disclosing a hairy chest, a pair of rather wrinkled slacks, and sandals over bare feet. He was carrying a coat over his arm.

Behind him was his mother, a woman of around fifty, not as tall as her son. She was rather dumpy and had a sharp pointed nose on each side of which alert brown eyes glittered as she made a quick appraisal of Mason; the eyes darted to Della Street, then around the office.

Behind Mrs. Hedley, Desere Ellis—slightly taller than average, her skin deeply tanned, honey-blonde hair, steady blue eyes and a figure a little on the spare side—seemed paled into insignificance.

"How do you do?" Mason said. "I'm Perry Mason."

The man, stalking forward and pushing out a hand, said, "I'm Fred Hedley. This is my mother, Rosanna, and my fiancée, Miss Ellis."

Mason nodded. "Won't you be seated?"

They found chairs. Desere looked at Della Street.

"My confidential secretary," Mason explained. "She takes notes on interviews, keeps things straight, and is my right hand."

Fred Hedley cleared his throat, but it was his mother who hurriedly interposed to assume the conversational initiative.

"Desere was told to come and see you," she said. "We gathered it was about her trust."

"I see," Mason said, noncommittally.

"We'd like to know about it," Mrs. Hedley said.

"Just what was it you wanted to know?" Mason asked.

Fred Hedley said, "The reason why Desere should be told to come and see you."

"Who told her?" Mason asked.

"The trustee, Kerry Dutton."

Mason's eyes locked with Hedley's. "Do *you* know him?" he asked.

"I've met him," Hedley said in a lukewarm voice. And

13

then added as though disposing of Kerry Dutton for all time, "A square, a moneygrubber. He's an outsider."

"He's a very dear friend," Desere Ellis interposed, "and my father had the greatest confidence in him."

"Perhaps too much confidence," Mrs. Hedley snapped.

"You see," Desere explained, "my father thought I was not to be trusted with money. There was rather a fair sum of money, and Father left it to Kerry as trustee so that I could have enough each year to keep me going for four years, but not enough to go out and splurge and wake up broke. I think Daddy was more afraid of my gambling than anything else."

"I see," Mason observed noncommittally, and then asked, "Do you have any predilection for gambling, Miss Ellis?"

She laughed nervously. "I guess Daddy thought so. I guess he thought I had a predilection for just about everything."

Mrs. Hedley said, "The reason we're here is that we understand the trustee has finally come around to the idea for an endowment."

"An endowment?" Mason asked.

"Fred's idea," she said. "He wants to have it so that—"

Fred Hedley held up his hand. "Never mind telling him the details, Mom."

"I think Mr. Mason should know them."

"Then *I'll* tell him," Hedley said.

He turned to face the lawyer. "Get one thing straight, Mr. Mason. I'm not a visionary; I'm not a goof. I play around with a bunch of poets and artists but I'm essentially an executive type."

Warming to his subject, he got up from the chair, leaned forward and placed his hands on Mason's desk.

"The trouble with our civilization," he said, "is that it can't develop itself. It tends to wash itself out.

"I think we are beginning to realize that every country needs to develop geniuses; but here in this country we can't do it because the genius can't develop; he starves to death.

"Look at the artists, the poets, the writers I know who could be developed into geniuses. I don't mean, Mr. Mason, that anybody has to develop them. All they need is to be left alone—just be free to develop their own talents."

"And they can't do it?" Mason asked.

"They can't do it," Hedley said, "because they can't make a living while they're doing it. They're starving to death. You can't develop anything on an empty stomach except an appetite."

"And you have some idea?" Mason asked.

"I want to endow up-and-coming poets, writers, artists, thinkers—principally, thinkers."

"What kind of thinkers?"

"Political thinkers."

"What kind of politics?" Mason asked.

"Now, there you go, Mr. Mason. You're trying to pin me down. Probably because of the beard. You think I'm a goof. I'm not. I go with a beat crowd, but I don't just want to drift along with the stream. I stay cool, but I want to *do* something."

"Such as what?"

"I want to *think*."

"You called Dutton a square," Mason said. "Why?"

"Because he *is* a square."

"What's a square?"

"He doesn't belong; he's narrow-minded; he's all wrapped up in a conventional concept of moneygrubbing.

"Times are changing. The whole world has changed. You can't get anywhere any more with the conventional type of thinking—not in art, not in writing, not in poetry, not in political thinking."

Mason glanced at Desere Ellis. "You are planning to finance this idea he has?"

"I wish I could," she said, "but I don't see how I can. As I told the Hedleys, Dad's money is just about used up. I wish now I hadn't been quite so extravagant. Sometimes I even wish Kerry Dutton had been more firm with me and had done more of what Dad wanted him to."

"In what way?" Mason asked.

"Not giving me money to throw away."

"You threw it away?"

She made a little gesture. "Oh, I was always taking off for Europe, or someplace, and buying new cars, new clothes, living it up. Once you start in, you can go through money pretty fast, Mr. Mason."

"And Dutton gave you the money?"

"I think his idea was that he'd take the money Dad left and pay it out in installments so that I would have a steady income until the time came when the trust was terminated."

"And then you'd have nothing?" Mason asked.

"Then I'd have nothing," she said. "Then I'd have to consider seriously how I was going to make a living."

"Did you remonstrate at all with Dutton?" Mason asked.

"Remonstrate with him?" she said, and laughed. "I remonstrated with him all the time."

"About giving you so much money?"

"About not giving me enough. I asked him how did he or anyone else know if I would live until the trust terminated. Why not go through life seeing what there was to see, living what there was to live, and then cross the bridge of the trust termination when I came to it."

Fred Hedley said, "If you ask my opinion, Mr. Mason, it was one hell of a way to handle a trust. Particularly, a spendthrift trust of that sort. Her father recognized that tendency in his daughter and wanted to guard against it. If Dutton had been on the job, we'd have a lot more money now for our foundation."

Mason smiled affably, the smile taking some of the sting from his words, and said, "But I didn't."

"Didn't what?" Hedley asked.

"Ask your opinion," Mason said.

Hedley flushed.

"Well," Mrs. Hedley said, "we're here. What do you have to tell us, Mr. Mason?"

"Nothing," Mason said.

"Nothing?"

Mason spread his hands in a gesture.

"Well, why are we here?" Fred Hedley asked.

"I thought perhaps *you'd* tell *me*," Mason said.

The trio exchanged glances.

Desere Ellis said, "Kerry Dutton called me last night. He told me that the time was approaching when the trust would be terminated, that he had retained you as his attorney and suggested that it might be a good plan for me to drop in and see you just to get acquainted."

"He suggested you bring the Hedleys?"

"No, that was my idea."

"Why," Mrs. Hedley asked, "would he need an attorney to terminate the trust if the money is all gone and—I suppose, of course, there will be accurate accounts submitted. Then all he has to do is to turn over whatever balance there may be and Desere will give him a receipt."

"Oh, there are lots of legal gimmicks in a thing of this sort," Fred Hedley said. "I can see why he thought he'd need an attorney, but I don't see why he wanted Desere to come in at this time."

"Perhaps it didn't occur to him that the three of you were coming," Mason said.

"Well, you may have a point there," Hedley admitted. "We thought, of course, from the way the message was received that you were going to make some announcement. There is, as I figure it, somewhere around fifteen thousand dollars left, and while that's not enough to carry out the plan we had in mind, it could be a start in the right direction. Desere, of course, would have to make some sacrifices, but she's going to have to anyway. Personally, I think it's a damn shame Desere frittered away all this money on frivolities when it could have served a really useful purpose."

"You estimate there's fifteen thousand dollars left?" Mason asked.

"In the trust? Yes."

"Just how do you figure?"

"Well, we know the amount of the original trust. We know what Desere has taken out and we can figure just about what the income should have been."

"How much have you been getting during the last twelve months?" Mason asked Desere. "I take it there's no secret about it."

"Heavens, no," she said. "I've had just about all of it." And then looking at him sharply, said, "You should know, as Kerry's attorney."

"I've just had one preliminary talk with him so far," Mason said. "I haven't gone into details."

"You're preparing an accounting?"

"Not yet."

"Well," she said, "I've been getting just about two thousand dollars a month for the past four years. But the last couple of months Kerry has intimated there will be a balance to be distributed on the termination of the trust. So I did a little figuring and believe there should be around fifteen thousand dollars—perhaps a little more—because Kerry has intimated there may be a little surprise for me."

"You haven't asked him specifically?"

"I haven't asked him much of anything," she said somewhat wistfully. "He calls me over the telephone and sends me checks and . . . he doesn't approve."

"Of what?"

"Of the Hedleys, for one thing," she snapped. "Of the way I do things, for another."

"Look here," Mason asked, "have you been spending two thousand dollars a month?"

"Not lately," she said; and then after a moment, added, "I'm running scared."

"What do you mean?"

"I'm trying to save a little."

"If you'd give up your apartment and live more simply, that last money that's coming in could go a long way toward getting Fred's foundation started," Mrs. Hedley said.

Desere Ellis shook her head. "I'm sold on it, but I'm going to use my money to take a business course and fit myself so I can make a living. I've been a playgirl long enough."

Fred Hedley looked at her in surprise. "You mean you're going to join the herd? You're going to become a keypounding square?"

"I'm mean that I'm going to fit myself to take the responsibilities of life."

"You would be simply a cog in a business machine," Hedley told her reprovingly. "In no time at all you'd lose track of your friends who are original thinkers. You'd become just another wage slave taking pothooks and slanting lines. You'd be on the outside."

Mason grinned. "Don't disparage secretaries, Mr. Hedley," he said. "They are pearls of great price and I can assure you that good ones are hard to find. These days you have to get them and train them over a long period of time. Miss Street is my right hand. I'd be lost without her."

"Wage slaves," Hedley snapped. "Human dignity is entitled to something more than machine routine."

Mason said, "Dignity means greatness. Look it up sometime."

He turned to Desere Ellis and said, "I don't know why Mr. Dutton suggested you come and see me. I am going to represent Mr. Dutton. I will be glad to talk with *you* at any time."

Mason placed a subtle emphasis upon the "you."

She nodded.

"But," Mason said, "I am acting as Dutton's attorney and at the moment I am not in a position to disclose anything about our relationship or about his affairs. I would want to have him present at any conversation with you."

"Heavens," she said, "you don't need to keep things confidential as far as anything in connection with the trust is concerned. It's dead open and shut. I've kept books on it; I know how much I had and how much I've spent."

"Were there any new investments?" Mason asked.

"I don't think so. Dad left the property in stocks and bonds. Kerry has had to sell them a little at a time to keep up my allowance, but there have been some dividends, some increases in value. That's part of the bookkeeping I've been doing—just checking up."

"We've gone back over the bonds and stocks," Hedley said, "and figured the dividends, interest payments and selling prices."

"I see," Mason commented noncommittally; and then

asked, "When are you going to enroll in this business course, Miss Ellis?"

"Tomorrow," she said.

Mason nodded approvingly and then, by his continued silence, indicated that he had nothing more to offer.

Hedley got to his feet and was promptly joined by Desere. Mrs. Hedley hesitated for a moment and then slowly arose from her chair.

"Thank you for calling," Mason said.

Della Street held open the exit door and they marched out.

When the door had closed, Mason turned to his secretary with a worried look. "I am probably violating all sorts of professional ethics," he said. "I'm afraid I'm getting swept along on the same current which has caused Kerry Dutton to lose his footing."

"Meaning you're falling in love with the girl?" Della Street asked, smiling.

Mason said, "I guess there's always the temptation to play God. . . . Here's a woman who has frittered away her life and, as far as she knows, all of the money that her father left her. She's tied up with some radicals who are writing intellectual poetry, espousing theoretical political views predicated upon limited experience and less knowledge; and she's now just at the point of coming to grips with herself."

"Well," Della Street asked, "what should you do? Tell her the truth?"

Mason said after a moment's thought, "I am not my client's conscience—only his lawyer."

Chapter 3

It was the next morning when Della Street handed Mason the folded newspaper as he entered the office.

"What's this?" Mason asked. "The financial page?"

"Right."

"What's the trouble?"

"Read it," she said. "Unless I'm mistaken, there's plenty of trouble."

Mason read the paragraph she indicated.

It was announced last night that Steer Ridge Oil & Refining Company had brought in a gusher proving up an entirely new territory in the Crystal Dome area. Market value of the company stock had been steadily declining and according to Jarvis Reader, president of the company, the news of this strike will reverse the downward trend. The new gusher is reported in an entirely new field which had previously been abandoned by one of the major oil companies as non-productive.

Mason gave a low whistle. "Better get our client, Kerry Dutton, on the phone, Della."

She nodded. "I looked up his number. I felt perhaps you'd want to call him."

She picked up the instrument, said, "Give me an outside line, Gertie." And then her fingers flew over the dial.

She held the phone for several seconds, then her eyebrows raised. She made a little gesture to Mason but she continued holding on for another ten seconds.

At the end of that time, she dropped the telephone back into place.

"No answer?" Mason asked.

"No answer."

Mason said, "Ring up my broker, Della. Tell him I want fifty shares of Steer Ridge Oil and Refining."

Della Street put through the call, transmitted the order, then said, "He wants to talk with you personally, Chief."

Mason nodded. "Put him on."

The lawyer picked up the telephone on his desk and said, "Yes, Steve, what is it?"

"You know something in particular or are you just playing a hunch on that paragraph in the paper this morning?"

"Well, it's a little of both," Mason said. "Why?"

"I don't know about that Steer Ridge stock," the broker said. "It's skyrocketed. Somebody apparently has been snapping up stock for the last few days and the thing has climbed sky high. It had been down to almost nothing."

"What do you know about the company?" Mason asked.

"Nothing much. It got along pretty well for a while; then the stockholders were reported to be fighting among themselves. There may be a proxy battle. A fellow by the name of Jarvis Reader is president. He's a queer sort of a duck, apparently a wild-eyed gambler who committed the company to taking up all sorts of leases on territory that had lots of acreage and not very much else. Under his management the stock has been steadily declining for some time. Recently someone started trying to get proxies.

"Now, whenever that happens in a low-priced stock the management tries to counter with news that will put the stock up in price. Hence a good reason for this paragraph in the paper; or they may *really* have a new field and the insiders have kept the news from the public so as to buy up stock; or it may be just a rumor.

"I was wondering if *you* have any inside information."

"Not me," Mason said. "I was hoping you had some."

"I've told you mine."

"Okay," Mason said, "buy me fifty shares at the market, regardless of what it costs. I want to be a stockholder in the company."

"Okay, if you say so," the broker said. "But I'd advise you not to go overboard simply on the strength of that newspaper report. That security has been a dog. A lot of people who had held it for years have sold out during the last year and some of them have taken quite a loss."

"Keep your eye on it," Mason said. "If there should be any really startling developments, let me know."

The lawyer hung up the telephone, glanced at Della Street, and said, "I wonder how our client is feeling about now?"

"That," Della Street said, "is a good question. Of course, he said he had the power to buy and sell, but the beneficiary *thinks* she has a block of that stock and that it's skyrocketing. On the strength of that feeling, she may be committing herself to all sorts of beatnik endowments."

The telephone on Della Street's desk rang.

Della Street picked it up, said, "Yes, Gertie?" Then after a few moments, said, "Just a minute. Have him wait on the line."

She turned to Perry Mason and said, "Fred Hedley is calling. He says that it's on a matter of the *greatest* importance and that he *knows* you will want to talk with him. He has some important information for you."

Mason hesitated a moment, then nodded and picked up his phone.

Della Street threw the switch which put both phones on the same line.

Mason said, "Hello. Perry Mason speaking."

Fred Hedley's voice was so excited that the words were all but telescoped together.

"Mr. Mason. Mr. Mason. I've got some wonderful news. This is *really* something! Have you seen the financial page of the morning paper?"

"What about it?" Mason asked.

"They've struck it rich. Steer Ridge Oil and Refining has proved up a new territory and brought in a big gusher."

Mason said, "This is Fred Hedley talking?"

"That's right, Mr. Mason. You remember me. I was in your office with my mother and Desere Ellis. I'm the one that's establishing the foundation."

"Oh, yes," Mason said. "What does the Steer Ridge Oil

and Refining Company have to do with your foundation, Mr. Hedley?"

"Everything in the world," Hedley said. "Some of the stock that's held in the trust for Desere Ellis is a big block of the Steer Ridge Oil and Refining. It's going up in value like a skyrocket."

"Well, that's interesting," Mason said. "How do you know it's still in the trust?"

"It has to be. That was the stock that Desere's father wanted Dutton to hang on to and sell only as a last resort."

"Was it a condition of the trust?"

"I don't know," Hedley said with a trace of irritation in his voice. "*You* should know. You're representing the guy."

"I am not familiar with the terms of the trust as far as *all* of the securities are concerned," Mason said. "I gathered from what you have told me that you were, and I was just asking the question. You folks told *me* he had distributed all but about fifteen thousand dollars. That means he must have had to sell some of the securities."

"Not the Steer Ridge," Hedley said confidently. "There's some sort of a proxy fight on, and a man called on Desere just a couple of weeks ago to get her proxies. She sent him to Dutton.

"That stock is going up like a rocket. It'll be worth thousands, hundreds of thousands!"

Mason said, "I fail to see just what difference all this makes—to you."

"This simply means there will now be adequate funds for us to carry out the work we want. Desere can give me the financial backing and I'll go to work on that endowment. It's going to be one of the biggest things in the whole world of creative art, Mr. Mason.

"Don't you understand what it's going to mean? My Lord, here are potential geniuses starving to death and being forced into some kind of a commercial treadmill occupation simply because they can't hang on until an unappreciative society recognizes their talent.

"We're going to create future Rembrandts. That is, they won't be stuffy like Rembrandt—they'll be truly creative in every sense of the word. We're going to develop writing geniuses. We're going to develop poets. We're going to emancipate American art and talent."

"Have you told Desere about this new development?" Mason asked.

"I haven't been able to get her thus far, but I certainly hope I can be the first to tell her. This was the day she started school, you know—business school."

"I see," Mason said. "Well, thank you very much for calling."

"Can you tell me where I can get in touch with Kerry Dutton?" Hedley asked.

"No," Mason said.

"I should talk with him right away in case he doesn't know about developments."

"You don't have his address?"

"I wasn't interested enough to ever ask for his address. Frankly, Mason, I think your client is a square, and I think he handled that trust like a fool."

"How should he have handled it?" Mason asked.

"He should have conserved the assets so there'd be enough money for Desere to do something that would really make a mark. Why, if he'd been careful and held her down to earth on expenses, she could have lived on just the income from the securities, and the principal could have been intact for something of this sort."

"All right," Mason said. "Thank you for calling but I'm not permitted to give out my client's address. I think the proper procedure would be for you to call Miss Ellis, have Miss Ellis call Dutton, and Dutton call me."

"All right," Hedley said, "if that's the way you want it. I was just trying to do you a favor."

"I appreciate your interest," Mason said. "Good-by." And the lawyer hung up.

Della Street, who had been monitoring the conversation and taking shorthand notes, looked up from her book and said, "Well, that's that. The fat seems to be in the fire."

Mason said, "Hang it, you have to sympathize with Dutton's viewpoint despite the fact it's irregular. However,

25

if it comes to a showdown on a strict legal basis, we can probably keep him in the clear.

"He had every right on earth to sell any securities that he wanted to and invest the money in other securities. He *didn't* have any right to mislead his beneficiary and he *should* have made accountings. He had no right to mingle his own funds with those of the trust. Somehow I have an idea that when Mrs. Hedley finds out about all this and finds out that the stock in the Steer Ridge Oil and Refining Company was sold a year ago, there's going to be a fine, large mix-up and I am going to be right in the middle of it."

"That," Della Street said, "seems to me to be the understatement of the week. What are we going to tell Desere?"

"The same thing we tell everybody," Mason said. "We are representing Dutton. We are not representing anyone else. We can give out no information. Let them get in touch with Dutton, and Dutton, in turn, will get in touch with me."

"When this news gets to him," Della Street said, "he'll— Well, he may take to the tall timber."

"How do you know he isn't there now?" Mason asked.

She looked at the lawyer for a long, thoughtful moment and then said, "That's right. We don't."

Chapter 4

Shortly after lunch Mason said, "Della, write out Kerry Dutton's name, address and telephone number on a card, will you please? And call Paul Drake at the Drake Detective Agency. Ask him if he can come in for a minute.

"Also, ring up my broker and make certain I am now a stockholder in the Steer Ridge Oil and Refining Company."

"If there's anything going on behind the scenes with inside information," Della Street said, "the insiders certainly had a wonderful opportunity for stock manipulation."

Mason said with a smile, "That's why I chose to become a stockholder, Della. As a stockholder of record, I'm entitled to protect my interests."

Della Street typed out the card with Dutton's address and telephone number; called the Drake Detective Agency, which was on the same floor with Mason; and a few moments later, Paul Drake's code knock sounded on the door of Mason's private office.

Paul Drake, head of the Drake Detective Agency, as tall as Perry Mason, broad-shouldered and good-looking, tried always to minimize his appearance.

He dressed in quiet clothes; always drove a car that was three to five years old—one of the more popular makes; and tried by every means to be self-effacing.

"Hi, beautiful," he said to Della; nodded to Perry; slid into the overstuffed, leather chair for clients and settled himself for a cigarette. "Shoot," he said.

"Paul," Mason told him, "this is on me. I want you to find a client. I am footing the bill."

"Client skipped out?" Drake asked.

"Could be."

"Owing you money?"

"No."

"Witness to something you want hushed up?"

"No."

"Witness to something in favor of one of your clients and you want his testimony?"

"No."

"What then?"

"Can't tell you," Mason said.

"Think he skipped out?"

"He could have."

"What do I tell him if I find him?"

"Nothing. Just let me know where he is."

"And I take it I'm not supposed to leave any back trail?"

"Try not to leave any back trail that leads back to me," Mason said. "Otherwise, you can go as far as you want. I realize that if you're going to get a guy located fast you can't go and ask questions without leaving *some* sort of a back trail. We'll have to take a chance on that."

"Starting now?" Drake asked.

"Yes," Mason said, handing Drake the typed card.

"You're in a hurry?"

"Yes. However, I have one other thing. This is something you should be able to get a routine check on. I want to find out something about Jarvis Reader, president of the Steer Ridge Oil and Refining Company."

"There was an article about them in the paper," Drake said. "Seems they struck it rich."

"You read that article, too?"

"Uh-huh. You can't believe too much of what you hear in deals of that sort, but I understand the stock is going up out of sight."

"You don't have any, do you, Paul?"

"Detectives don't get rich buying and selling stock. They don't get rich, period."

"Okay," Mason told him. "On your way, and let's see what you can turn up. Keep me posted."

Less than fifteen minutes after Paul Drake had left the office, the telephone on Della Street's desk rang, and Della

28

Street, answering it, said, "All right, tell him to sit down a moment, Gertie. I'll see if Mr. Mason can see him."

Della Street turned from her telephone. "Speaking of angels," she said, "Jarvis Reader is in the outer office."

"He wants to see me?" Mason asked.

She nodded.

"Go bring him in, Della."

Della Street said, "Tell him Mr. Mason will see him, Gertie. I'm on my way out to get him."

Della Street left the office to return a moment later with a powerful, somewhat stoop-shouldered man in his middle fifties. He had a weather-beaten face, bushy eyebrows, piercing gray eyes, and a belligerent manner.

"Hello," he said. "You're Mason?"

Mason grinned. "You're Reader?"

"Right."

"What can I do for you?"

Reader said, "You're representing Kerry Dutton, I understand."

"Who told you that?"

"Never mind. I want a straight answer. Are you or are you not representing Kerry Dutton?"

"Mr. Dutton has retained me to represent him in one matter. Yes."

"In *one* matter?"

"That's right."

"Well, there are going to be several matters."

"Such as what?"

"I have learned," Reader said, "that Dutton made statements that I was crooked; that my management of the company was manipulated for my own purposes; that I didn't know straight up about oil; that I was primarily interested in bilking people into investing in stock so I could keep myself in power as the head of the company at a darn good salary."

"When did you hear all this?" Mason asked.

"Some time ago, but I haven't done anything about it because I wanted to wait until I could prove what a liar Dutton was.

"Now then, my management has been vindicated, and I'll bet Dutton wishes he had the twenty thousand shares of stock he sold a while ago."

"Sold it?" Mason asked, inquiringly.

"That's right. That's when he made the statements. He was reported to have sold the stock to a purchaser and warned him that it probably wasn't any good; that I didn't know straight up about the oil business; that I was just working a flimflam getting a lot of sterile acreage tied up so I could make a big showing to people who knew nothing about the oil business and keep drawing a nice salary, having an expense account, a private airplane and all that sort of stuff."

"If," Mason said, "you're really intending to sue my client, you shouldn't be talking with me, and I certainly am not going to talk with you. You can get an attorney and have him call on me if there's anything you want to adjust."

"I don't need an attorney," Reader said. "Not right away. I'm not here to sue. I'm not here to threaten. I'm simply here to tell Dutton that I will accept an apology—a public apology which I can print in the papers."

"Why don't you tell him?" Mason asked.

"Can't find him. He's hard to catch."

"You've tried?"

"I've tried. . . . I wanted to be the first to tell him about our oil strike before he read it in the papers. I couldn't find him. Then the news was released on the radio and the papers picked it up. Now he's heard all about it and I'm the last person in the world he wants to see."

Mason said, "Just as a matter of curiosity and not talking about any claims you may have against Mr. Dutton because I don't care to discuss them, you folks were friendly at one time?"

"Friends!" Reader exclaimed, drawing a forefinger across his throat. "Oh, yes, we're friends. That guy has done everything he could to make it tough for me."

"What I meant was that you knew him?"

"Hell yes, I knew him."

"And have for some time?"

"Ever since he became trustee under that will. I went to him and wanted him to invest more money in Steer Ridge Oil. He laughed at me. I'll bet he wishes now he'd followed my advice. That trust would have been worth a lot of money today.

"I was friendly with Templeton Ellis. He had faith in me. He was one of my first backers. He put money into Steer Ridge on four different occasions; left a tidy block of stock, and just because it started going down in value, that smart-aleck trustee sold it out. Not only sold it out, but shot off his big mouth that the management was crooked; that no one in the company knew anything about the oil business and that I was getting leases on land that nobody else would touch with a ten-foot pole."

Reader paused for a moment, then went on, "Now, there's something else you'd better know about if you're getting yourself tied up with Dutton: The beneficiary of that trust thinks he still has the twenty thousand shares of Steer Ridge stock in the trust. She doesn't know he sold her out."

"What makes you think that?" Mason asked.

"I don't think, I know. I'll tell you something else. Dutton will be frantically trying to buy that stock back. He's willing to pay almost any price for it. I'm personally going to see he can't get it back.

"When you see him, tell him that I know everything he's doing. And tell him that his stool pigeon, Rodger Palmer, who's trying to pick up stock and proxies, isn't going to get to first base.

"I've forgotten more about corporate management of oil properties than these birds ever knew. . . . Tell Mr. Kerry Dutton that whenever he's ready to buy a page ad in the daily papers apologizing to me, I'll think about letting him off the hook. Until that time, he can fry in his own grease."

Mason smiled. "I think you'd better tell him that yourself, face to face, Mr. Reader."

"I will if I can find the guy."

Reader turned on his heel and started for the outer office,

paused to say, "And when Desere Ellis finds he's sold her out, there's going to be hell to pay."

"You can go out this way," Della Street said, holding open the exit door.

Reader hesitated a minute and said, "Thanks, I'll go out the same way I came in. I like it that way."

He strode out through the door to the entrance room.

Chapter 5

It was after seven-thirty. Mason and Della were closing up the office, and Mason was just holding the exit door open for Della when the unlisted phone rang stridently.

Mason said, "That's the unlisted telephone. That'll be Paul Drake."

Della Street nodded and hurried across to the instrument, picked it up and said, "Yes, Paul?"

She nodded to Mason, who picked up the extension phone on his desk.

"Hi, Paul," Mason said. "What's new?"

"This fellow Dutton is something of a problem, Perry."

"What about him?"

"He's being hard to find."

"I didn't think he'd be easy or I wouldn't be paying you fifty dollars a day to look him up."

"Well, he's trying to be *real* hard to find. Someone is looking for him and I have an idea that someone is a process server with some papers to put right in the middle of Dutton's hot little hand."

"And you think Dutton's hiding out to avoid that?"

"He's hiding out to avoid something."

"Where are you now, Paul?"

"I'm in a telephone booth across the street from a service station about four blocks from Dutton's apartment. I have an idea I'm going to pick up his trail. While I was waiting I thought I'd telephone for instructions."

"How come?"

"Well, I became pretty well convinced he wasn't intending to go back to his apartment. There's a man sitting outside waiting. I looked up the license number on his car. He's a chap named Rodger Palmer. From the way he acts,

I think he's a process server. He's sure anxious to see Dutton and he has lots of patience. He's just covering the entrance to the apartment house. Also, the girl at the switchboard said Dutton had been in and out several times earlier in the day, carrying a big brief case each time."

"Both in and out?" Mason asked.

"Both in and out."

"Could be he was moving stuff out and stashing it in the trunk of his automobile," Mason said.

"That's the point," Drake said. "I figured he'd buy his gasoline around here somewhere, so I covered all the gasoline stations around and finally not only hit pay dirt but I may have hit a jackpot, as far as Dutton is concerned. I found the place where he buys his gasoline and has the service work done on his car. The car is there now being serviced. He told the attendant to change the oil, give it a good lube job and check all the tires—that he was going on a long trip."

"Didn't say where?"

"No, but the car is there and I have a stakeout on it."

Mason said, "I want a line on Dutton, Paul. I'm mixed up in something with him and I may be skating on rather thin ice, ethically. A great deal depends on what kind of a guy he is, whether he's on the up-and-up or whether he's taking people for rides."

"Well, I think he's getting ready to skip out."

"All right, sit on the job," Mason said. "Follow him and find out where he's headed."

"How strong do I go?"

"As strong as you have to."

"Suppose he heads out of town?"

"Head out of town right after him, Paul."

"I'll probably need some help."

"Get it!"

"Suppose he buys a plane ticket and heads for Brazil?"

"Get the plane; get the flight number; wire your correspondent in Brazil and pick him up when he lands."

"In other words, the sky's the limit."

"That's right. But what with his having the car serviced

and all of that, you can be pretty sure he's going to start out by automobile."

"And you want me to stay with him?"

"Like glue," Mason said.

"Okay," Drake told him. "I'll be reporting. I'll need at least one assistant on the job. I'll phone for one now."

Mason hung up the phone and faced Della Street with a puzzled frown.

"How much are you mixed in all this, Chief?" she asked. "I mean, how deep?"

"Let's put it this way," Mason said, "Dutton tells me he's embezzled money from the beneficiary of the trust. The way *he* tells it, he's made restitution; and the way he *says* he did it, it was technically legal within the terms of the trust, provided he told me the truth about the trust.

"But the way he's acting doesn't coincide with his story to me. Unless you have something on for tonight, Della, let's go tie on a nosebag, then come back to the office and sit around for a while. I have an idea we may have a showdown somewhere along the line. We'll keep in touch with Paul Drake's office and let them know where we are."

Della Street smiled. "If you can promise an extra cut of rare roast beef for me, with baked potato, onion rings and a green salad, I'm with you until midnight."

"We'll double it," Mason said. "I know just the place where they specialize in that kind of food."

Chapter 6

Halfway through the meal, the waiter approached the table and said, "You're accepting calls, Mr. Mason?"

"Yes, I told the headwaiter when I came in," Mason said.

The waiter nodded, and plugged in the telephone. Mason picked it up and heard Paul Drake's voice.

"Where are you now, Paul?"

"The office told me where you were," Drake said reproachfully. "I'm sitting in my automobile munching on a candy bar to keep my stomach from getting corns where it rubs against my backbone, I'm that hungry."

"What's the score?"

"Well, I picked up Dutton, all right."

"Where did he go?"

"Right now, he isn't going anyplace. He's sitting in a car, watching."

"What's he watching?"

"He followed a guy here who looks like a dressed-up beatnik."

"Tall, broad-shouldered, with a beard?" Mason asked.

"That's the fellow."

"And where is the place he's waiting?"

"It's the Doberman Apartments on Locks Street. Does that mean anything to you?"

"It means quite a bit," Mason said. "That's where Desere Ellis lives, and the man with the beard is probably calling on her."

"And Dutton is checking?"

Mason thought for a moment; then said, "No. Dutton probably is waiting to be sure the coast is clear when he talks to Desere Ellis. He probably has decided to tell her something rather important and he wants to be certain he isn't interrupted. The beatnik's name is Fred Hedley. He tries to ape the crowd and be a cool cat. Actually he wants to promote a deal with Desere Ellis whereby he can play God to a lot of artists, poets and writers.

"I can tell you that much, but it's in confidence.

"If my hunch is right, Paul, Dutton will wait there until Fred Hedley comes out and drives away. Then Dutton will go on up to the apartment."

"Then what?"

"When Dutton comes out," Mason said, "shadow him. Have you got a relief yet?"

"I had a little difficulty getting an operative I could trust," Drake said, "but I finally got one and he's on his way here. My men are tied up today. That is, the good men.

"I went out on this job myself, because the man I first sent out reported he couldn't get any trace of Dutton. I didn't like to hand you a failure, and I figured there'd be a lead if a man put in enough time looking for it. So I went out and started covering the service stations. I hit pay dirt there and got stuck with the job."

Mason said, "Get a relief. Put the finger on Dutton and go get a good dinner. Be sure you get a good man."

"The one I have coming is okay," Drake said.

Mason said, "We're going to be here at this café for another half hour; then we'll go up to the office and wait for your call there. Try to give us a report by ten-thirty, because we'll knock it off shortly after that."

"Okay," Drake said, "will do."

Mason hung up the phone and related what he had learned to Della Street.

She made a little grimace.

"Meaning?" Mason asked.

"Meaning that Desere Ellis is or has been infatuated with Hedley and that's not the way things should be. I'm pulling for Dutton."

"And so?" Mason asked.

"So," she said, "Dutton is waiting for Hedley to go home. As soon as Hedley leaves, Dutton will go up to Desere Ellis' apartment and she'll know intuitively that he was sitting outside waiting for Hedley to go home. That puts two strikes against Dutton as far as any woman is concerned. A woman wants a man who will chart his own course and assert himself; not one who will skulk in the shadows and wait until the coast is clear before he makes a move."

"Of course," Mason pointed out, "it may be that Dutton isn't afraid to face Hedley for a showdown, but he's planning to tell Desere the whole business and he doesn't want Hedley to know about Desere's financial affairs."

"In that case Fred Hedley's mother will step into the picture and things will move fast after that," Della Street said. "That is, if she has an idea there's more money in the trust than appears to be the case at the present time."

Mason raised his wineglass. "I give you the Mexican toast," he said, *"salud y pesetas y amor sin suegras."*

"What is that?" Della Street asked.

"That," Mason said, "is a toast that Mexican gentlemen give to each other in the privacy of their clubs."

"What does it mean?"

"It means health, wealth and love without mothers-in-law."

Della Street burst out laughing. "The man who invented that must have known Mrs. Hedley," she said.

"Or someone pretty much like her," Mason agreed.

They finished a leisurely dinner, and Mason was just signing the check when the waiter came hurrying up with the telephone. He plugged it in and said, "An emergency, Mr. Mason."

Mason picked up the phone, said, "Yes. What is it?"

Drake's voice said, "You'd better get up here, Perry. Quick!"

"Where is here?"

"That address I gave you, the Doberman Apartments. If you want to protect your client, you'd better get here. There's hell to pay."

"We'll be right there."

"I'll be waiting," Drake told him. "I'll be at the front of the apartment house. It's on Locks Street."

"Coming right away," Mason said.

Mason grabbed Della Street's arm, "Emergency," he told her.

"What's happened?"

"Paul didn't say. Just said we'd better get up there, quick, if we wanted to protect our client. Come on, let's go."

Mason signaled the headwaiter, who in turn signaled the doorman, and the lawyer's car was in front waiting by the time Mason and Della Street reached the outer door of the restaurant.

Mason, an expert driver, jockeyed for position at the traffic signals, but they encountered some heavy traffic and it was some twenty minutes before they reached the address.

Drake was waiting for them on the curb.

"Well," he said, "you're too late."

"What happened?" Mason asked.

Drake said, "The fellow with the beard came out, got in his car and started off. Just as you had predicted, Dutton didn't follow him. He jumped out of his car and hurried into the apartment house.

"Now, I don't know whether Hedley knew that Dutton was waiting and wanted to trap him, or whether Hedley had forgotten something, but Dutton hadn't been in the house five minutes when Hedley came driving back, double-parked his car, jumped out and went into the apartment house like a guy carrying the mail."

"And what happened?"

"Plenty," Drake said. "A woman ran out on a balcony on the third floor and started screaming for the police. I guess someone telephoned. . . . Anyhow, a police radio patrol car came driving up, and about that time Dutton came out of the apartment. He was hurrying, but he took one look and saw that police car and his gait slowed to a saunter and he came idling across the street while the cops jumped out of the radio car and went dashing into the apartment house."

"Then what?"

"Dutton drove off and—"

"Hang it, Paul," Mason said, "I wanted Dutton followed."

"He's being followed. I had a relief here. I thought I'd make a report myself because the relief wouldn't have any opportunity. They were going—fast."

"What happened?"

"Well, I talked with one of the cops when they came out. They had Hedley with them, but Hedley was pretty much the worse for wear. I think he's going to have a sore nose for a couple of days and there's blood all over his shirt. He's also got one eye swelling shut, and the way he talked, his lips were pretty well puffed up.

"As nearly as I can get the story, Hedley started the brawl. He caught Dutton up in this girl's apartment and there were words, and then Hedley took a swing and from that point on the party got rough."

"And Hedley got the worst of it?" Mason asked.

"Well, he certainly didn't get the best of it. Dutton didn't have a mark on him, but Hedley looked as if he'd been put through a washing machine."

"What did the cops do?"

"They turned him loose after they got him outside, but I heard enough of the conversation to learn that they figured he was the one who started it."

"What was Hedley saying?"

"He was going to swear out a warrant for Dutton's arrest for assault and battery and anything else. The officers didn't seem too much impressed, however, and told Hedley he'd better pick up the tab for damages on the apartment of a Miss Ellis in 321, or he might find himself facing trouble."

Mason turned to Della Street, who was smiling broadly.

"Well, Della," Mason said, "I guess things turned out the way you wanted them to, and on that note, since the crisis seems to have passed, since Dutton is being tailed, we'll call it a day."

"And," Della Street said, demurely, "thank you for a lovely dinner."

"Dinner!" Drake said. "That damn candy bar has been repeating on me for the last hour."

Mason said, "I suggest the café where you reached us, Paul. It has wonderful extra-cut rare roast beef, baked potatoes, onion rings and salad. And, of course, since you're still on duty, the cost of the dinner would be an acceptable expense in the eyes of the Bureau of Internal Revenue."

Drake's eyes were anguished. "A couple of hours ago," he said, "I could have eaten a live horse. Now, with the taste of that synthetic chocolate in my mouth, I don't want anything except a glass of warm milk and later on a little bicarbonate of soda."

Chapter 7

The next morning Mason stopped in at Paul Drake's office on the way down the corridor to his own office.

The receptionist said, "Mr. Drake's down in your office, Mr. Mason, waiting to see you on an important matter. He telephoned Miss Street and she said you were expected in about this time so he went down to wait."

"I'll go on down," Mason said. "But tell me first, where's our quarry?"

The girl at the telephone desk smiled and said, "I'm not supposed to know, but Mr. Drake received a telephone call from Ensenada, Mexico, just before he telephoned Miss Street."

"That," Mason said, "will make a nice vacation."

The lawyer was smiling as he walked down the corridor and opened the door of his private office.

"Good morning, Della," he said. "Hi, Paul, how are you? I've been thinking we're working too hard. How would you folks like to break away from routine for a day and drive down to Ensenada, Mexico?

"That's a wonderful Mexican city, wonderful food, sweet lobsters, the *caguama*, or big turtle from the Gulf, enchiladas, chile con carne, refried frijoles, ice cold Mexican beer—"

"Hush," Della Street said, "you're breaking Paul's heart. He had stomach trouble last night."

"How come?" Mason asked.

Drake shook his head. "I knew when I was getting into this business what the occupational hazards were. Like a surgeon who lives under tension and usually develops heart trouble by the time he's fifty-five, a detective lives on hamburgers and bicarbonate of soda. . . . How the devil did you know about Ensenada, Perry?"

"Stopped in your office on the way down," Mason said. "Your telephone operator told me you had a call from Ensenada."

"Well," Drake said, "my man lost Dutton."

"Lost him!"

"That's right."

"For how long?"

"About an hour."

"What happened?"

Drake said, "My man who relieved me took up the tailing job."

"And what did he do?" Mason asked.

"Well, Dutton left the apartment house just as the cops came up. He drove around aimlessly for a while; then after about ten or fifteen minutes stopped at a service station and—"

"I thought you said his car was filled up," Mason said.

"That's right, he'd filled it up where he had it serviced, but this time he was only interested in the telephone. He went into the telephone booth and dialed a number. My man had to be a little careful. He parked across the street and watched with binoculars but he couldn't get the number.

"Anyhow the fellow either got the wrong number or a busy signal, because he just held the phone to his ear for a few seconds; then hung up, waited a few seconds, then dialed again."

"What happened this time?"

"Well, my man figured that telephone conversation was pretty damn important. He wanted to get it the worst way, so he took a chance."

"On what?"

"He approached the booth while the fellow was in there, acting as though he wanted to make an important call. Dutton waved him away, but my man had one of those pocket battery-powered wire recorders and some adhesive tape. I've been using them lately and they work pretty well.

43

He had parked his car around the back of the booth and he ostensibly walked back to wait by his car. What he actually did was fasten the wire recorder on the back of the booth, using adhesive tape, and then he got in his car and drove away. He didn't drive very far but waited where he could watch Dutton's car.

"When Dutton came out of the booth after that last call, he was going like a house afire. My man figured he'd retrieve the wire recorder later on or ring the office and tell somebody to go and get it. He stayed with Dutton."

Mason nodded. "That was the thing to do."

"But Dutton drove like crazy. He went through three red lights that my man followed him through, hoping that a traffic officer would tag both of them. On the fourth red light, Dutton almost had a collision. The intersection was blocked. Dutton got away and my man was stymied by traffic."

"Going through red lights that way, didn't Dutton know he was being followed?"

"Probably," Drake said. "He may even have been trying to shake pursuit, but somehow the way my operative felt, Dutton was going someplace in too much of a hurry to give a hoot about anything—and that's the way it turned out."

"Go on," Mason said.

"Well, after my man lost him and knew he'd lost him for good, he went back to the phone booth and picked up the wire recorder, turned back the wire recorder to the starting point and then listened to the conversation. Of course, he could only hear one end of the conversation. It was brief and to the point."

"What was it?" Mason asked.

"The first thing Dutton said was a question. 'What's new? You know who this is.' Then he waited for the answer and then said, 'I called the other number and was told to call you at this pay station. . . . I'll pay over the five thousand if you're acting in good faith.' Then there was a period of silence while he was evidently getting instructions, and then he said, 'Give me that again . . . the seventh tee at the Barclay Country Club, is that right? . . . Why pick that sort of place?' Then he said, 'All right, all right, it's nearly that time now. . . . Yes, I've got a key. . . .' Then he hung up the phone and that was the end of the conversation."

"Your man followed up that lead?" Mason asked.

"My man went to the Barclay Country Club. It's a key job, and my man didn't have a key, and at that hour of the night there wasn't any chance of getting in without one, but there were three or four cars parked and one of them was Dutton's. My man checked the license number."

"So what did he do?"

"Put himself in a position where he could pick up the car when it left, and waited it out. He got there at ten minutes after ten o'clock."

"How long did he have to wait?"

"About twelve minutes."

"Then what?"

"Then Dutton came out at ten-twenty-two and started driving south. My man tailed him without headlights for a while and it was pretty damn risky. But Dutton stopped after a short distance and got out of the car. My man went on past, then pretended to have tire trouble, jacked up the car and waited until Dutton came sailing past.

"Dutton drove to the border, kept on driving down to Ensenada. He had no idea he was tailed. He's staying at the Siesta del Tarde Auto Court. He is registered under the name of Frank Kerry."

Mason said, "He doesn't need any credentials in the way of tourist cards or anything of that sort as long as he's no farther south than Ensenada, eh, Paul?"

"That's right. If he gets below Ensenada, he's going to need a tourist card or an entry permit of some kind; but as far as Ensenada he's on his own."

"Your man still tailing him?"

"That's right. He's doing the best he can. Of course, one man isn't much good on a twenty-four-hour-a-day job. . . . Do you want me to send a relief down?"

Mason was thoughtful. "Might as well, Paul," he said.

"And I think the time has come for me to assume the role of a Dutch uncle."

"Doing what?" Drake asked.

"Getting this thing cleaned up before I get too deeply involved," Mason told him. "After all, Dutton is a client of mine but— Well, I may have to insist that he surrender himself or go to the police."

"And then what?"

"Then," Mason said, grinning, "*I'll* try to beat the rap."

The lawyer turned to Della Street. "How," he asked, "would you like to take a couple of notebooks, plenty of pencils, a briefcase and a quick trip down to Ensenada, Mexico? This time I think we'll get the real story."

Chapter 8

Mason and Della Street left Tijuana behind, took the smooth, new road to Ensenada.

"The old road," Mason said, "was more scenic."

"Wasn't it? But these days one sacrifices everything to speed. However, it's nice to get where you're going without fighting the steering wheel around a lot of curves. Do you think he's really embezzled money, Chief?"

"I don't know," Mason said. "The way he acts, I'm afraid he's leaving me to hold the sack."

"In what way?"

"There'll be a hue and cry," Mason said, "and I'll be in there pitching, assuring everybody that things are going to work out all right; that I have every confidence in my client; that I know the facts; that I have advised him and that he hasn't committed any crime; that in due course everything will be explained and cleared up."

"And then?" she asked.

"And then," Mason said, "after a while it may dawn on me that my client is being hard to find."

"You mean in Ensenada?"

"Ensenada," Mason said, "could be simply the first stop. He's going to stay there long enough to get out from under the telltale registration of his automobile and all that. He'll probably leave the car where it can be found; double back to the United States; grab a plane for Brazil or someplace, and leave me behind to make explanations."

"You think he's that kind?" she asked.

"No," Mason said shortly, "I don't."

"Then what?"

"That," the lawyer told her, "is the reason we're making this trip, Della."

They drove into Ensenada, threaded their way down the busy main street, and Mason asked directions to the Siesta del Tarde.

"Will you know Drake's man?" Della Street asked as they drove up in front of the auto court.

"*He'll* know *me*," Mason said.

The lawyer got out and stood stretching and yawning, looking around at the scenery, soaking up the sunlight, before helping Della from the car.

The two of them walked toward the office of the auto court, then paused and looked back toward the car. Mason caught the eye of the man who was sauntering down the street.

The man winked at Mason, put a cigarette in his mouth, fumbled through his pockets and said, "Pardon me, could you let me have a match?"

"I can do better than that," Mason said. "I have a Zippo lighter."

The lawyer snapped the lighter into flame, held it toward the man with the cigarette.

"In Unit nineteen," the detective said. "He hasn't been out, unless he sneaked out while I was telephoning a report to Los Angeles.

"That's his car over there, the Chevy with the license number, OAC seven, seven, seven."

"Okay," Mason said, "we're going in and talk with him. Keep an eye on things. I may want you as a witness. . . . How are you feeling? Pretty well bushed?"

"Staying awake is the hardest part of a job like this, Mr. Mason. I was up all night and sitting here in the car where it's warm, I kept wanting to take forty winks. If I had, I'd be apt to wake up and find the bird had flown the coop."

Mason said, "You can either check out within the next thirty minutes, or we'll have a relief for you. Paul Drake got in touch with a relief operative in San Diego this morning and he's on his way down."

"That'll help," the detective said. "I'm not complaining, I'm just trying to stay awake and sometimes that's just about the hardest job a man can have."

"Okay," Mason told him, "we're going in."

The lawyer nodded to Della Street.

A long driveway led to the office; then down to a parking place by the cabins. Palm trees and banana trees shaded the units of the court.

Mason, ignoring the sign which said *Office*, guided Della to the unit occupied by Kerry Dutton.

The lawyer turned to his secretary and said, "When I knock on the door, say, 'Towels.' "

The lawyer knocked.

A moment later, Della Street said, "Towels."

"Come in," a man's voice called, and a hand on the inside turned the knob on the door.

Mason pushed his way into the room, followed by Della Street.

Kerry Dutton stared at them in speechless amazement.

Mason said, "When I'm representing a person, I like to do a good job, and in order to do a good job I have to have the *real* facts. I thought perhaps you could tell me a little more about your problem."

Dutton's eyes went from one to the other.

Mason moved over to a chair; held it for Della, then seated himself in the other chair, leaving the bed for Dutton.

Dutton's legs took him over to the bed and seemed to give way as he settled down on the counterpane.

"Well?" Mason asked.

Dutton shook his head.

"What's the trouble?" Mason asked.

"It isn't what you think," Dutton said.

"How much of what you told me was untrue?"

"What I told you was generally true," Dutton said. "It was the things I didn't tell you that—oh, what's the use?"

"There isn't any," Mason assured him. "That is, no use in trying to hold out on your lawyer. Sooner or later the facts will come to light, and if your lawyer doesn't know what they're going to be in advance, he's pretty apt to be caught at a disadvantage."

Dutton simply shook his head.

"Now then," Mason went on, "no matter how legal your actions may have been in the first place, you weakened your position by resorting to flight. In California, flight is considered evidence of guilt, and a prosecutor is permitted to introduce that evidence in a criminal trial."

Dutton started to say something.

There was a knock on the door.

Dutton looked at Mason, then at Della Street, apprehension on his face.

"Expecting visitors?" Mason asked.

Dutton got up from the bed, started for the door, stopped.

The knock was repeated, this time in a more peremptory manner.

"Better see who it is," Mason said.

Dutton opened the door.

Two men came in; one in the uniform of a police officer, one in plain clothes.

The man in plain clothes sized up the occupants of the room, bowed, and said, "The señorita, I hope, will excuse me. I am the *Jefe* of *Policia*. May I ask which one of you gentlemen is Kerry Dutton from Los Angeles?"

"And the reason for the request?" Mason asked.

The chief of police regarded him with appraising eyes. "I do not think," he said pointedly, "that I have the honor of your acquaintance, sir."

"I am Perry Mason, an attorney at law," Mason said, "and this is my secretary, Miss Della Street."

The chief bowed deferentially. "It is such a pleasure to make your acquaintance, sir, and I am so sorry that I have to interfere with what was perhaps a professional conference—no?"

"That is right," Mason said. "I am conferring with my client, and my secretary was preparing to take some notes. If you could spare us perhaps a half an hour, I am quite certain that we will be at your service at that time."

The eyes softened into a smile. "That is what you would call a good try, but unfortunately, Señor Mason, the business that I have with Mr. Dutton is of the urgency."

He turned to Dutton. "Señor Dutton, it is with great regret that it is necessary for me to inform you that you are in custody of the *policia*."

"And the charge?" Mason asked.

"A warrant of first-degree murder which we will honor here to the extent of declaring that Señor Dutton is an undesirable alien. As such, we will escort him to the border and ask him to leave Mexico immediately."

"Murder!" Mason exclaimed. "Who was killed?"

"That information will, I trust, be forthcoming when Señor Dutton reaches the border. It is my unpleasant duty to see he is promptly escorted to the border."

"And at the border?" Mason asked.

The officer smiled. "At the border," he said, "I feel quite certain that police from your country will be waiting. What would you do if you were a police officer in the United States, and you knew that a man whom you wished to arrest for murder was to be deported as an undesirable alien?"

"That procedure seems a little high-handed to me," Mason said.

"Doubtless, it does," the officer announced, "but we do things in our country the way we wish to do them in our country, just as you are permitted to do things in your country the way you wish to do them in your country. That is, we do not interfere with you and we do not care to have you interfere with us.

"I am going to ask you to withdraw, if you will please be so good."

Mason said, "I am an attorney at law. My client is accused of a crime and I demand the right to represent him and consult with him."

The chief smiled. "You are an attorney in the United States?"

"Yes."

"And in Mexico?"

Mason hesitated.

"In Mexico," the chief of police went on, "attorneys in good standing are referred to as *licenciados*. That means they have a license granted by the Mexican government to practice law. You perhaps have such a license, Señor Mason?"

Mason grinned. "All right, it's your country, your customs and your prisoner."

"Thank you," the chief said, "and there is no reason why we should detain you further, Señor Mason."

"But this man is charged with murder," Mason asked, "and his attorney can't talk with him?"

The chief shrugged his shoulders. "You are licensed in your country. You can talk with your client there at any time. Here he is charged only with being an undesirable alien. We do not wish undesirable aliens in our country any more than you do."

"What's undesirable about him?" Mason asked.

The chief smiled and said, "He is a fugitive from justice in the United States. This makes him very undesirable as a Mexican visitor."

"There are legal proceedings looking to his deportation?" Mason asked.

"Only the proceedings necessary to get him transferred to the border. Here in Mexico we expedite the process of justice as much as possible."

Mason looked at Dutton, then back at the chief of police. "Zip the lip," he said.

The chief raised his eyebrows. "I'm afraid I didn't understand you."

"Pardon me," Mason said, "it was just a bit of American slang."

"Oh, yes—you Americans. And now, Señor, if you and your so charming secretary will just step this way, please—and I strongly recommend the restaurants here. You will find the service excellent and the food beyond compare. As tourists, we will try to make you happy."

"But not as an attorney?" Mason asked.

The chief shrugged expressive shoulders. "Unfortunately, you are not an attorney in Mexico. If you would reside in Mexico and comply with the requirements, I have no doubt but that you could become a *licenciado*, but until then . . ."

There was another expressive shrug of the shoulders.

The police officer held the outer door open.

Mason put his hand on Della Street's arm, and together they stepped out of the room into the shaded walkway which was filled with the sound of white-winged doves, the scent of flowers and the beauty of semitropical foliage.

Chapter 9

As Mason and Della Street walked down the little sidewalk in front of the auto courts, Drake's detective came running toward them, motioning frantically.

Mason quickened his step.

"What is it?" he asked.

"I called Drake to report, and he's on the phone. Something he wants to tell you about right away. Says it's terribly important; that I should get you. He's going to hold the line until you can come."

Mason nodded to Della Street, hurried down the walkway under the palms and banana trees, his long legs making the detective trot to keep up, while Della Street made no attempt to match the pace.

In the phone booth, where the receiver was off the hook, Mason closed the door, picked up the receiver, said, "Yes? Hello."

Drake's voice said, "That you, Perry?"

"Right."

"All right," Drake said, "there's a rumble. I don't know how bad it is as far as your client is concerned, but it's pretty bad at this end."

"Murder?" Mason asked.

"Right. How did you know?"

"The officers moved in on Dutton while I was talking with him."

Drake said, "Here's all I know. An early golfer found a body on tee seven at the Barclay Country Club. The man had been shot once."

"Did they find the weapon?" Mason asked.

"I don't know," Drake said. "This much I do know. An attempt had been made to keep the police from identifying

54

the victim and apparently that attempt has succeeded to date.

"Everything in the man's pockets had been taken. There isn't so much as a handkerchief. The labels had been cut from the inside of the coat pocket and on the little hanging strap at the back of the neck.

"The cutting had been skillfully done with a very sharp knife or a razor blade.

"The time of death hasn't been officially determined as yet, but it could be at just about the time our man tailed Dutton out to the golf club—that's within the general overall time limit that they've mapped out for the murder. After they have a complete autopsy, they may let Dutton off the hook. Right now I understand the tentative time is fixed between nine-thirty last night and two-thirty this morning."

"All right," Mason said. "Now, your man couldn't get into the club because it was a key job?"

"That's right. You have to go in through the clubhouse to get to the course."

"There must be a service road," Mason said.

"There is, somewhere. I haven't looked it up."

Mason said, "At that hour of the night, the murdered man probably let himself in with a key. It's a cinch that Dutton did."

"Dutton's a member of the club," Drake said.

"All right, probably the other man is, too. Get photographs from the newspaper reporters and start covering members who are regular players and—"

"We're way behind on that," Drake said, "the police have five detectives interviewing all the members whose record of greens fees shows that they've been playing regularly. They have photographs of the dead man and they're trying to make an identification."

"Have you seen a photograph?"

"No," Drake said. "I have a general description."

"Shoot."

"A man about fifty-five," Drake said, "with dark hair, powerful broad shoulders, slightly stooped, black eyes, about six feet one inch in height, weight two hundred and five pounds, very hairy hands, big powerful wrists."

"No keys on him?" Mason asked.

"No keys, no coins, no knife, no handkerchiefs, no pens, no pencils—nothing."

Mason said thoughtfully, "Paul, you talked about a man you thought was a process server who was waiting to serve papers on Dutton?"

"That's right, he—By George, Perry, it *could* be the same man. The description fits."

"You'd recognize the man if you saw him?"

"Sure."

"Stay away from the morgue," Mason said. "Let's see if you can get a look at the police photographs."

"Gosh, Perry," Drake wailed, "if I make the guy, I'll have to go to the police. That's evidence a private detective can't withhold."

"You can't make a positive identification from a newspaper photograph like that," Mason said. "You'd have to see the corpse."

"Well, you were talking about police photographs."

"I was," Mason said. "Now I am talking about newspaper photographs.... Della and I are on our way back just as fast as we can get there. I'll leave my car here. I'll get my friend Munoz to fly us to San Diego. You have Pinky waiting at the San Diego airport with a twin-motored job to bring us in to the Tri-City Airport, and sit tight until we get there. Meet us at Tri-City Airport."

"Even if there's a very good resemblance in the newspaper photographs, I'd have to run it down," Drake said. "In a murder case my license wouldn't be worth a thin dime if I held out an identification."

"You and your license," Mason said.

"Me and my living," Drake told him. "I'll have the plane in San Diego by the time you get there."

"We'll get there pretty darn fast," Mason said and hung up.

Chapter 10

"Pinky" Brier, the famous aviatrix, brought the twin-motored plane in at the Tri-City Airport as gracefully as a bird coming in to a landing.

A worried Paul Drake, who had been anxiously waiting, came out of the late afternoon shadows to meet Perry Mason and Della Street as they disembarked.

"You left your car?" Drake asked.

"Left it down there," Mason said. "We'll get it later on. Right now we're working against time."

"We're working against time and against a condition you aren't going to like," Drake said.

"What's the condition?"

"I've seen the photograph in the papers."

"What about it?"

"Perry, I *think* that man is the one that I took for a process server—perhaps he is, perhaps he isn't, but in any event, he was hanging around keeping cases on this Dutton apartment."

"But you can't make a positive identification from a newspaper photograph of that sort," Mason said.

"I know I can't, but I've got enough of an identification to tell Lieutenant Tragg that I might be of some assistance and should go down to the morgue and take a look at the body."

"Then, if you identify him," Mason said, "you're going to have to tell Tragg where you saw him and when."

"That's right."

"And that," Mason said, "is going to put our client in a hole."

"Your client is in a hole now," Drake said.

"Well, you'll put him deeper in the hole."

"He's in just about as deep as he can get right now," Drake said, "or he will be when my operative testifies.

"You remember my operative was shadowing Dutton. He put a wire recorder up against the telephone booth and heard one side of the conversation in which Dutton arranged to meet someone out at the Barclay Country Club on the seventh tee.

"That's where they found this murdered man."

Mason said thoughtfully, "Your operative is in Ensenada now?"

"No, he's started home," Drake said. "By the time he gets here he'll know what his duty is. He'll report to the police, and the police will confiscate that wire recording."

"Who has the wire recording?"

"He does. It's in the trunk of his car.

"You've got a responsibility here, too, Perry. You can't suppress evidence. You can represent your client regardless of what the evidence against him may be, but you can't conceal evidence of a murder."

"All right," Mason said, "let's face it before they smoke us out. Let's call Lieutenant Tragg. Then Pinky can take us in to the Los Angeles Airport, and Tragg can meet us."

Drake said, "We'll have cars scattered all over the country. Your car in Ensenada; mine here at Tri-City."

"We can rent cars if we need them," Mason said, "but we're fighting against time. Della will drive your car to Los Angeles."

"What does your client tell you?" Drake asked.

"Nothing," Mason said.

Drake said, "The only defense that's going to be open to you in the long run is trying to prove self-defense. Your client went out there to meet this guy. Whoever it was, the man was blackmailing Dutton. The party got rough. Your client had to shoot to kill in order to get away. The police found five thousand dollars in fifty-dollar bills in your client's possession when he was arrested at the border. They think this was money for a blackmail payoff."

"That's what they *think*," Mason said. "How do they know it wasn't getaway money?"

"They believe it was a blackmail payoff. They know things we don't know."

"I suppose so," Mason said. "There's so much about this that I don't know that it bothers me. The best defense is the truth, but in this case I don't know what the truth is, and I'm not at all certain my client is going to tell me."

"Why not?"

"There's just a chance he's protecting someone, or trying to."

"That would mean a woman, wouldn't it?" Drake asked.

Mason said, "Come on, let's get hold of a telephone."

Mason went to a telephone, called the Los Angeles Police Department, got Lt. Tragg at Homicide on the line.

"I see you're investigating a death at the Barclay Country Club," Mason said.

"You saw that in the papers?"

"I heard it was in the papers."

"Yes. Yes," Tragg said, "and I suppose you have some information in connection with it that you've been sitting on for several hours, and now that you've decided it's too dangerous to hold out any longer, you've decided to be cooperative."

"You do me an injustice," Mason said, grinning.

"I know. I always do," Tragg said dryly.

"As a matter of fact," Mason told him, "I have just this minute arrived by plane from Mexico. I have been talking with Paul Drake, and Paul Drake tells me that from the picture of the murdered man that was published in the paper he has an idea he may have seen the individual in question sometime last night."

"Where? When?" Lt. Tragg asked, snapping the questions like the crack of a whip.

"Not so fast," Mason said. "We don't know as yet that it's the *same* person."

"Well, you'd better find out, and find out pretty damn quick," Lt. Tragg said. "If Paul Drake has any information that's going to help us clear up a murder case, he'd better get it in our hands fast."

"That's what we want to do," Mason said. "We're even

going to charter a plane and fly in to the airport. We'll meet you there in about half an hour. We'll go to the morgue with you. If it turns out it's the same man, Drake will be only too glad to give you all the information you want."

Tragg said, "We're bringing a suspect in for questioning on that murder. Do you suppose there's any chance—of course, I know it's only a one-in-a-million shot—but is there any chance, Mason, that this man is a client of yours?"

"The victim?"

"No, the one we're bringing in."

"Well, that would depend," Mason said, "on the identity of the man you're bringing in."

"His name," Lt. Tragg said, "is Kerry Dutton. He's a young man who's had quite a spectacular success as an investment counselor."

"What connects him with the murder?" Mason asked.

Tragg said, "I had my question in first. Is he, by any chance, a client of yours?"

"He's a client of mine," Mason said.

"That," Tragg said, "explains a lot. Where are you now?"

Mason told him.

"You think you can get here within twenty-five or thirty minutes?"

"Yes. We have a twin-motored plane all ready to go."

"Get in it, and get started," Tragg said. "I'll meet you personally with a radio car at the airport, and I want one-hundred-per-cent co-operation— Now, get that, Mason, I want one-hundred-per-cent co-operation. We're not playing tiddlywinks. This is murder."

"We'll meet you there," Mason said.

Mason hung up the phone. "How bad is it?" Drake asked.

"Just as bad as Tragg can make it if things don't work out so well."

"And if they do work out well?"

"It's just about as bad as I could make it for my client," Mason said.

"Well, there's one advantage about giving the officers the

information they need to clinch a case against someone," Drake pointed out, "they don't catch you unprepared."

They gave Pinky only time enough to finish a cup of coffee; then were flown in to Los Angeles where Lt. Tragg met them.

"All right," Tragg said, "start talking."

"We have to go to the morgue before we talk," Mason said. "We don't *know* that this is the same person."

"You tell me what the highlights are on the way," Tragg said, "and then if it turns out to be the same person, we won't lose any time; and if it isn't the same person, I'll keep the facts in confidence."

"I'm sorry," Mason said, "we can't do that. It's a matter of a professional obligation to a client."

Tragg said, "Under those circumstances, you boys can prepare yourselves for a ride. We're going places very, very fast. You'd better strap yourselves in with those seat belts, because they might come in handy. And hang onto your hats."

The trip to the morgue was made in record time. Lt. Tragg and the officer who was with him led the way into the big, silent room where the wall was lined with steel drawers, looking for all the world like some huge sinister filing cabinet.

The officer knew the number without looking it up, took hold of the handle and pulled out the sliding cabinet.

Drake stood looking at the corpse for nearly ten seconds.

"All right," Tragg said at last, "is it or isn't it?"

Drake looked at Mason and shrugged his shoulders, then turned to Tragg. "It is," he said.

"All right," Tragg said, "let's get started. We've lost enough time already—perhaps too much."

Drake said, "I had the job of shadowing Kerry Dutton yesterday."

"Go on."

"Someone else was on the job."

"Who?"

"This man," Drake said, indicating the still form on the slab.

61

"What do you know about him?"

"Nothing. I thought he was a process server."

"He was tailing Dutton?"

"He was waiting for Dutton. That is, he was casing Dutton's apartment and I had an idea he was a process server."

"What gave you that idea?"

"Just something about the way he acted."

"All right," Lt. Tragg said, "I don't want to pull it out of you a piece at a time, minutes are precious. We're trying to build up a case and we don't want to get the wrong man but we sure do want to get the right one."

"I can't tell you much about him," Drake said, "except I can give you the license number of his automobile. I looked it up and have the owner's name."

Tragg's face lit up. "What was the license number?" he asked.

Drake pulled out his notebook and gave Tragg the number and the name of Rodger Palmer.

Tragg dashed to the telephone, exploded into action, telephoned orders to trace the license application, to wire in a descriptive classification of the thumbprints, and to check identities.

When he had finished, he returned to where Drake and Perry Mason were standing.

"Just why were you shadowing Kerry Dutton?" Tragg asked.

Drake started to say something, caught Mason's eye, hesitated; then said, "Because Perry Mason told me to."

Tragg flushed. "Let's not try any run-arounds," he said.

"That isn't a run-around," Mason said. "It's a straightforward answer. That's all Paul Drake knows about it."

"All right, then I'll ask you. Why did you tell Paul Drake to shadow Dutton?"

"That," Mason said, "is something I'm not at liberty to disclose."

Tragg said, "You'll disclose everything you know about the murder, or you'll find yourself in hot water up to your necktie."

"I'll disclose everything I know about the *murder*," Mason said.

"Well, what you know about Dutton fits in with what we know about the murder."

"I don't think it does," Mason said. "As a matter of fact, I was having Paul Drake shadow Dutton because I was worried about my own responsibility in the matter."

"So I gathered," Tragg said. "You don't ordinarily have a detective agency shadow your own clients."

"Sometimes I do."

"Now then," Tragg said, "here's the important question, and I want an answer to it. Did any of this shadowing take Kerry Dutton to the vicinity of the Barclay Country Club?"

There was a period of silence. Then Mason said cautiously, "I believe I should answer that question. I can state that it did."

"The hell it did!" Tragg said, his face lighting up. "At what time?"

"What time, Paul?" Mason asked.

"Right around ten-ten to ten-twenty," Drake said.

"Now then," Mason volunteered, "in order to keep you from feeling you're having to draw information out of us a bit at a time, I'm going to tell you that before Dutton went out to the country club he had a conversation with someone and apparently arranged to meet that person out at the country club."

"How do you know?"

"He went into a telephone booth and called someone. One of Drake's men was shadowing him. He put a wire recorder on the outside of the telephone booth and walked away. It's a very sensitive recorder, compact but highly efficient. After Dutton drove away, Drake's man came back and picked up the recorder, ran it back, found out what the conversation was about and went out to the Barclay Country Club."

"He didn't follow Dutton out?"

"No, Dutton went through red lights and generally drove like crazy. So, after trying to follow him, Drake's man went back and picked up the recorder, ran it back to the starting point, listened to the conversation, and was able to make out that an appointment had been made at the Barclay Country Club."

"And he drove out there right away?"

"Yes. He went right out there."

"And Dutton's car was out there?"

"That's right. Dutton's car and two or three other cars."

"Was one of them this car that you gave me the license on?" Lt. Tragg asked Drake.

"I don't know as yet, but we will know," Drake said.

The telephone rang—a sharp strident sound in that room of eternal silence.

Tragg strode over to the instrument, picked it up, said, "Yes ... speaking."

The officer listened for several seconds; then a slow grin spread over his face. "That does it," he said. "Okay."

Tragg hung up and said, "All right, we've got our corpse identified. His name is Rodger Palmer all right. He was an employee of Templeton Ellis until Ellis died; then he went to work for the Steer Ridge Oil and Refining Company.

"Now then, do any of those activities tie in with what you fellows know?"

Mason chose his words carefully. "Templeton Ellis was the father of Desere Ellis. Kerry Dutton is the trustee of money which was payable to her under her father's will. Some of the stocks, I believe, which were included in the estate at one time were shares of the Steer Ridge Oil and Refining Company."

Tragg turned to Drake. "What's the name of your detective, the one with the wire recorder?"

"Tom Fulton."

"Where is he now?"

"On his way up from Ensenada."

"Where's he going to report when he reaches the city here?"

"To my office."

"I want to see him as soon as he reports," Tragg said, "and I want to be very, very certain that nothing happens to that recording. That is evidence in the case and I want it."

"You'll have it," Mason promised.

"Getting facts out of you two," Tragg said, "is like pulling hen's teeth with a pair of fire tongs, but thank you very much for your co-operation."

"We gave you what we had," Mason said.

"You gave me what you *had* to give me," Tragg amended, "but I appreciate it just the same. It's bad business when we can't get a corpse identified."

"But even without the identification, you felt you had a case against Kerry Dutton?"

Tragg grinned and said, "We brought him in for questioning."

Mason said, "They told me down in Mexico that he was under arrest; that there was a warrant out for him, charging first-degree murder."

"Tut, tut," Tragg said.

"You didn't extradite him?"

"We couldn't have extradited him without preferring a charge."

"But he is under arrest?"

"He's been brought in for questioning."

"He's my client," Mason said. "I want to see him."

"If he's charged with anything, you can talk with him. As soon as he's booked, he can call an attorney."

"Where is he now?" Mason asked.

Tragg said, "I'll put it on the line with you, Perry. As far as I know he's between here and there."

"There meaning?"

"Tecate," Lt. Tragg said, grinning. "It was a lot easier for us to pick him up there than it would have been in Tijuana, so when the Mexicans deported him as an undesirable alien, they put him back into the United States at Tecate."

Mason turned to Paul Drake. "Okay, Paul," he said, "let's go to the office. Della should be there by now with your car."

"Better hang around your office," Tragg said. "If Kerry Dutton wants to call you, we'll give him *one* telephone call."

"One should be enough," Mason said.

Chapter 11

Perry Mason and Paul Drake found Paul's car in the office parking lot. "Your man Fulton, Paul?" Mason asked.

"What about him?"

"You know what about him. We've got to get in touch with him."

"He's on his way home from Ensenada. Police will be laying for him and want to grab that wire recording."

"I know they will," Mason said. "We've got to get to him before the police do."

Drake shook his head. "What do you mean?" Mason asked. "You mean it can't be done?"

"I mean it's not going to be done," Drake said. "I have a license to consider. We can't play hide-and-seek with the police in a murder case. You're a lawyer; you know that."

Mason spoke slowly, giving emphasis to each word as he enunciated it. "Paul, I'm an attorney. I have a license, the same as you do. I'm not going to suppress any evidence. You're not going to suppress any evidence. We're not going to tamper with evidence, but I'm representing a client. The police are going to try to convict that client of first-degree murder. They're moving pretty fast in this thing. That means there's some evidence that we know nothing about. I want to find out about it. I want to know what it is. Your operative is going to be a witness for the prosecution. We can't help that, but we sure have a right to get a report from him at the earliest possible moment. You're paying him, and I'm paying you. Now then, what kind of a car is he driving? What route is he going to take?"

Drake shook his head. "I don't like it."

Mason said, "You don't have to like it. I know what I'm doing. I'm not asking you to violate any law."

66

"Well," Drake said, reluctantly, "there's a service station out on the corner of Melwood and Figueroa. It's a big service station with plenty of pumps and employees on duty, and every operative who has been on a long, out-of-town trip is instructed to fill his gas tank at this station when he comes in.

"The big thing in the private detective business is to be sure you don't run out of gas when you're on a tailing job.

"The man who runs that service station knows most of my operatives. I know he knows Tom Fulton. We can ask him if Tom has been in there yet. If he has, it means that Tom has parked his car and reported to the office and the cops have probably grabbed him by this time, or, at any rate, they will before we can get hold of him now."

"There's a phone booth, Paul. Put through the call."

Drake entered the phone booth, put through the call, came back and shook his head, "He hasn't been in yet. You can't tell just when he will come in. The guy has been up all night on a tailing job and it's a long drive from Ensenada up here. He was entitled to get some sleep."

"The police will have a stakeout on your office, Paul, and I don't dare take any chances. You're going to have to go down to that service station and wait— Hang it, we'll both go. They probably have a stakeout on my office as well as on yours. They may figure we'll try to head Fulton off. Come on, Paul, we'll just have to go and wait."

Drake drove through traffic and into the service station. He caught the eye of the manager. "Going to wait around a while, Jim," he said.

"He hasn't been in yet," the manager said, looking curiously at Perry Mason.

"We want to speed matters up as much as possible," Drake said. "He's a witness, and we want to—"

"Put him in touch with the police at once," Mason interpolated.

"Okay, there's parking room over there next to the grease rack," the man said. "Make yourselves comfortable. You any idea when he's going to be in?"

"He'll be in shortly," Drake said.

Drake backed the car into the space so that they had a commanding view of the gas pumps.

"Want to phone Della Street and let her know where you are?" Drake asked.

Mason shook his head. "We'll keep everyone guessing for a while."

An hour and a half passed; then Drake suddenly gripped Mason's arm. "Here he comes, Perry," he said. "Now, remember we can't do anything that will serve as a peg on which the police can hang a complaint."

Mason's eyes were wide with candor—too wide. "Why, certainly not, Paul! We're only co-operating with the police. Call him over."

While the attendant was putting gasoline in Fulton's car, Drake caught his eye and called him over.

"Why, hello, Mr. Drake. What are *you* doing here?"

"Waiting for you," Drake said.

"Gosh, I'm sorry. I took just a little shut-eye down in Ensenada before I pulled out. I was afraid I couldn't keep awake and—"

"That's all right," Drake said.

The operative's eyes twinkled. "You certainly get around, Mr. Mason."

Drake said, "He wants to ask you a few questions."

"Go ahead."

Mason said, "You lost Dutton last night on the tailing job?"

"That's right. He drove like crazy. He went through signals, right and left and darn near got me smashed up trying to follow him. I was hoping we'd both get pinched and I could square the pinch by explaining to the officer. It's a chance we have to take."

"And how did you pick him up again?" Mason asked.

"He went to a phone booth and I bugged the phone booth with a little bug that fits right up snug against the glass with a rubber suction cup. A transistor wire recorder is suspended underneath."

"And what did you find?"

"He said he was going out to the Barclay Country Club

and would meet someone on tee number seven. I've reported all that."

"I want it official this time," Mason said. "You didn't
spot him out there?"

"Not right away. His car was there."

"You tried to get in?"

"I tried the door to see if it was unlocked."

"Was it?"

"No. There was a spring lock on it."

"So you waited?"

"That's right."

"How long did you wait?"

"Twelve minutes."

"And then what?"

"And then he came out."

"How did he act when he came out, excited?"

"He seemed to be—Well, he was in a hurry. He knew
exactly what he wanted to do."

"He didn't pay any attention to you?"

"I was sitting pretty well in the shadows back in my car.
That is, I'd crawled over in the back seat so I wasn't at all
conspicuous."

"There were other cars parked around there?"

"Half a dozen, I guess."

"You didn't take the license numbers?"

"No, I spotted Dutton's car there, and he was the one I
was tailing so I didn't pay any attention to the others—no
one told me to."

"That's all right," Mason said. "We're not blaming you,
but can you describe the cars?"

"Why, they were just—just ordinary cars."

"No car that stood out, not a sport job, or some big
flashy job?"

"No, as I remember it, they were all rather mediocre—I
took them for cars belonging to employees who slept in on
the premises. There weren't too many of them—I guess
three would just about hit it, but there may have been four."

"All right," Mason said, "we don't have much time. We

have to hit the high spots. Dutton came out, got in his car and drove away?"

"That's right."

"You tailed along?"

"Yes."

"Any trouble?"

"Just once. I started following him with my lights off. Dutton stopped his car rather suddenly and then backed up. There was nothing for me to do but to keep on going."

"So you lost him again?"

"No, I didn't lose him. I got down the road, pulled off to one side, put out a red blinker, got out a jack and jacked up the rear bumper. I made as if I was changing a tire. I kept my eye on him all the time."

"How far away was he?"

"Oh, half a mile, I guess."

"His lights were on?"

"Yes."

"You couldn't see him, you could only see the headlights?"

"That's right."

"He just stopped?"

"Yes."

"Then what happened?"

"Well, then he got in his car and went on."

"What did you do?"

"I stood there helpless and let him pass. Then when he got ahead of me, I let the car down off the jack fast, threw the jack in the rear seat, jumped in and took off after him. In a case of that sort the subject hardly expects a crippled car to come to life and take off after him, so he isn't suspicious."

"And you tailed him, how far?"

"All the way to the border and then on to Ensenada."

"Did he make any stops?"

"Once for a cup of coffee and a hamburger."

"What did you do?"

"Sat outside the place, parked in my car, and drooled," the detective said. "That coffee looked so darn good, I would have given a week's pay for a cup, but I didn't dare let him spot me so I had to sit outside and wait until he came out."

"Do you think he knew he was being tailed?"

"I don't think so. I would drop behind for a way and then come up, and I passed him once or twice where I could keep his headlights in my windshield and pulled in to a coffee joint as though I was getting coffee, but as soon as he passed me I took up the chase again."

"Now, that wire recording," Mason said, "you have it?"

"Yes."

"The police want it."

"I wondered if they would. I was going to ask Drake what to do with it."

Mason said, "Go to the office. Don't tell anyone that you have seen either Drake or me unless you are asked specifically. If you are asked by the police, don't lie. Tell them that I was waiting for you and that I told you I wanted you to take your evidence to the police at once; that they were anxiously awaiting it."

"I don't say anything about Mr. Drake?"

"Not unless they ask you specifically. If they ask you if you've talked with anyone, tell them you talked with me. If they ask you if anyone was with me, you can tell them Paul Drake was, but just don't volunteer any information. On the other hand, appear to be very cooperative."

Fulton nodded.

"Now then," Mason said, "why did Dutton bring his car to a stop and back up? Any idea?"

"No, I haven't," Fulton said, "but I checked on my odometer."

Mason's face brightened. "You did?"

"That's right. He was on Crenmore when he stopped, exactly one and three-tenths miles from the entrance to Barclay Country Club."

Mason turned to Paul Drake. "Paul," he said, "get this man a bonus of the best dinner in the city for himself and his wife— You married, Fulton?"

"Not yet," Fulton said, grinning. "I was, but it didn't take. I played the field for a while and now I'm getting ready to go overboard again. This time it's going to be different."

"Get your girl friend and take her to the best restaurant

in town," Mason said. "Get everything you can eat, have a bottle of champagne with dinner and turn in the bill on your expense account."

Fulton shot out his hand. "That's mighty fine of you, Mr. Mason."

"I always like to see a good job well done," Mason said.

Fulton looked at Drake. "Anything else?"

Mason shook his head.

"Okay," Fulton said, "I'll be on my way. I'm to go in to the office and start making out a report in the usual way?"

"That's right," Drake said. "Take a typewriter and start tapping it out."

"Do I say anything about the subject stopping there on the road?"

"You sure do," Mason said. "Don't conceal *anything*. Remember, those are my instructions. Don't conceal a single piece of evidence from the police."

Fulton signed the ticket for the gasoline and drove out.

"Well," Drake said, "I guess we may as well—"

"Go to that culvert and see what's there," Mason interjected.

"Culvert?" Drake asked.

"Sure," Mason said. "That's why he stopped and backed up. We'll take a look at whatever is in that culvert."

"And then what?"

"Then," Mason said, smiling, "we don't touch anything. We call Lieutenant Tragg and tell him that Fulton reported to us that the subject had stopped a mile and three-tenths from the country club; that we went out to see what had caused him to stop and back up. Much to our surprise, we found a culvert. We looked in the culvert and it appeared that something had been stashed in there and so we're calling the police."

"Tragg will be hopping mad," Drake said.

"Let him hop," Mason pointed out.

"Suppose there isn't a culvert? Suppose it was something in the road?"

Mason said, "I'm willing to bet ten to one it was a culvert."

72

"Suppose the police have checked it?"

"They could very well have done so," Mason said. "Whenever a crook has evidence to dispose of, he looks for the first culvert he comes to, and if Lieutenant Tragg is as smart as I think he is, he has probably instructed his men to look at the first culvert on every road leading away from the country club."

"In which event he will have been one jump ahead of us."

Mason grinned. "But only one jump, Paul. Come on, let's go. If you don't mind, I'll drive. We don't have much time."

Mason drove to the country club, checked the odometer, turned and drove a mile and three-tenths.

"Well, you're right," Drake said. "It's a culvert."

"You can see marks where a car was braked to a sudden stop," Mason said. "Well, we'll take a look, Paul."

The lawyer parked the car, got out, raised the hood of the car, took a flashlight from the glove compartment, and walked down the embankment to the culvert. He looked up and down the road, said, "Let me know when the coast is clear, Paul."

"Okay," Drake said, after two cars had passed, "you've got an open road now."

Mason dropped to his knees, peered into the culvert.

"See anything?" Drake asked.

"Footprints," Mason said, "and nothing else."

"Car coming, Perry."

Mason hurriedly arose, walked over to the side of the road.

A passing motorist stopped. "Having trouble?" he asked, noticing the upraised hood.

"Just a vapor lock," Mason said, smiling. "I think it will straighten itself out if we let it cool off a minute. Thanks!"

The motorist waved his hand. "Good luck," he said, and drove away.

Mason thoughtfully lowered the hood of the car, got in, and started the motor.

"Now what?" Drake asked.

"Now," Mason said, "I'm going to try and see my client— and ask him what it was he concealed in that culvert."

Chapter 12

Mason sat looking across the dividing partition at his client's worried face.

"How much did you tell them?" Mason asked.

"Not a thing," Dutton said. "I told them that I resented the way they had made the arrest and taken me out of Ensenada; that I thought I had been kidnaped by the police; that I was indignant, as a citizen, and I put on the act of being too damn mad to co-operate."

"It's all right," Mason said. "It's a good act. The only thing is, it doesn't fool anyone. What have they got on you, do you know?"

"No."

"They've got something," Mason said. "Suppose you tell me the real story."

"I wanted to tell it to them," Dutton said, "but I was going to follow your instructions because you're my attorney. If I'd told it to them, I'd have been free by this time."

"You think you would have?" Mason asked.

"Very definitely," Dutton said. "They don't have a thing on me."

"Well, tell me your story," Mason said, "and if I'll buy it, I'll have you pass it along to the police and the district attorney."

"There isn't much to tell," Dutton said.

"Did you know the dead man?"

"I've talked with him on the phone. That is, if he's Rodger Palmer."

"What do you know about him?"

"Not too much. But he had me in kind of a peculiar position."

"Blackmail?"

74

"Well, not exactly. Palmer was engaged in a sneak attack on the management of Steer Ridge Oil and Refining Company. He wanted to get rid of the management and put his own crowd in."

"You knew that?"

"I knew that—at least, he told me."

"Go ahead," Mason said. "What happened?"

"Well," Dutton said, "Palmer knew that Desere Ellis had a big block of stock in the oil company. At least, he assumed she did. He knew that her father had bought it and that it had gone into the trust fund."

"And so?" Mason asked.

"And so he went to Miss Ellis and wanted her to give him a proxy. She told him that she couldn't do it because the stock was in my name as trustee. So then he asked her to write a letter to me as trustee, instructing me to give him a proxy on stock."

"And she did?"

"She did."

"And then?" Mason asked, his eyes showing his keen interest.

"Then, of course, I was in a spot," Dutton said. "I didn't have the stock. I didn't want her to know I didn't have the stock. That would have caused her to ask for an accounting. Therefore, I didn't want to tell him I'd sold the stock."

"This was at a time when the value of the stock was low?"

"That's right. It was just before the strike in the new field. Palmer could have bought up control of the company if he could have found the stock and had the money, but he was working on a shoestring."

"So what did you do?"

"I told him I would have to know more about what he had in mind, and what his plans for developing the company's property were before I'd honor Miss Ellis' letter.

"He insisted on seeing me; I refused to give him an interview. Then he played his ace in the hole. He told me he had something to tell me about Fred Hedley. He said it would eliminate Hedley from the picture as far as Desere

Ellis was concerned. He said he needed money to carry on his proxy campaign and that if I'd bring him five thousand dollars in fifty-dollar bills, he'd give me an earful of facts on Hedley that would put Hedley out of circulation."

Mason regarded his client skeptically. "And he also wanted proxies?"

"Yes."

"He was a blackmailer then?"

"I guess that's the word for it. However, I'd have done *anything* to prevent Desere marrying Hedley."

"What about proxies?"

"That's the strange, incredible thing," Dutton said. "When he made me that offer, I decided to take him up. I went out and bought up twenty thousand shares of Steer Ridge Oil stock in my own name. I got them at from ten to fifteen cents a share. I intended to let Palmer think they were the original shares of stock from the trust.

"Then within a couple of days the new strike was made and the stock started climbing sky high."

"And the stock is in your name, and not in the trust?"

"That's right."

"You have no letters from Palmer, no evidence to back up your story?"

"No."

Mason shook his head. "Tell that story to a jury and add it to your handling of the trust fund and you'll be crucified."

"But I did what I felt was best."

"For whom? For you or for Desere?"

"For everyone."

Mason shook his head. "A jury will think you sold out the Steer Ridge Oil stock from the trust fund; that you had a tip the new wells were in oil sand; that you acted on that tip to feather your own financial nest; that Palmer found out what you were doing, or rather what you had done, and was blackmailing you."

There was dismay on Dutton's face. "I hadn't thought of it that way."

"Better start thinking of it that way now," Mason said.

"Good heavens, *everything* I've done can be misinterpreted," Dutton said.

"Exactly," Mason agreed.

"You, yourself, don't even believe me," Dutton charged.

"I'm trying to," Mason said. And then added, "That's part of my job. A jury won't have to try so hard."

There was an interval of grim silence, then Mason said, "So you agreed to meet Palmer surreptitiously at a spot that wasn't particularly convenient to pay over blackmail, but was ideal for murder."

"He was the one who picked the spot," Dutton said.

"Too bad he can't come to life long enough to tell the jury so," Mason observed.

"Why in the world did you ever consent to go out there to meet him?" Mason asked after a few moments.

"That's where he wanted me to meet him."

"Why?"

"He didn't say why, but I gathered that he had to be pretty furtive about what he was doing. He didn't want it to come out into the open that he was trying to round up proxies on the stock or get control of the corporation. He wanted to get himself pretty firmly seated in the saddle before he turned the horse loose and let it buck. And he seemed afraid to let anyone find out he was selling me information."

"All right, you agreed to go out there," Mason said, wearily, "and you went out there."

"That's right."

"For your information," Mason told him, "the police have a wire recording of your conversation from the telephone booth. The one in which you agreed to go out there. You—"

The lawyer stopped before the expression of utter consternation on Dutton's face.

"How in the world could they get a wire recording of *that* conversation?" Dutton asked.

Mason regarded the man with thought-narrowed eyes. "It seems to give you a jolt."

"Good heavens, yes. Of course, it gives me a jolt. I

77

picked out a telephone booth and— Wait a minute, there was some fellow snooping around on the outside."

"He planted a bug and a wire recorder," Mason said. "I thought you should know it."

Dutton lowered his eyes, then suddenly raised them. "He bugged the conversation in the telephone booth, he didn't tap the line?"

"No," Mason said. "Wire tapping is illegal."

"I see," Dutton said. "Then he only has my end of the conversation recorded on wire?"

"That's right."

"Just that end of the conversation?"

"That's right, but your end was pretty incriminating. You said that you would go out there and meet him on the seventh tee at the Barclay Country Club."

"Yes, I did," Dutton said, slowly, "and the police have that recording?"

"The police have that recording."

Dutton shrugged his shoulders.

Mason said, "All right, Dutton, you've stalled around now long enough to have thought over all the angles. You've had plenty of time to think up a pretty good story; you have an idea of what the police have against you, so why not try to give *me* the facts? The *real* facts might help."

"He was dead when I got there," Dutton said.

"How long did you hang around?"

"Too long!"

"Why?"

"I had a key to the clubhouse," Dutton said. "All members have keys. Palmer knew that. He'd borrowed a key from a friend. Palmer wasn't a member. I went in through the clubhouse, out the back door to the links and walked down to the seventh tee. That's about a hundred yards from the clubhouse.

"All the time I was walking down there, I thought I was making a darn fool of myself. That was no way to meet a man and carry on a legitimate business conversation or a legitimate business transaction."

"You can say that again," Mason observed dryly.

"What do you mean?"

"If it embarrasses you to tell me about it," Mason said, "think how you're going to feel when you have to tell twelve cold-eyed, skeptical jurors about it and then be cross-examined by a sarcastic district attorney."

There was a long moment of silence.

"You may as well get on with it," Mason said.

Dutton said, "I stood around the seventh tee expecting to see Palmer there. I was, of course, watching the skyline for a man to show up. After some ten minutes, I started walking around and then I saw something dark on the ground. At first I thought it was a shadow. I moved over and my foot struck against it."

Dutton stopped talking.

"Palmer's body?" Mason asked.

"It was Palmer's body."

"What did you do?"

"I got in a panic. I almost ran back to the clubhouse; got in my car and drove away."

Mason said, "You didn't have a flashlight?"

Dutton hesitated a fraction of a second, then said, "No."

"You went out there in the dark?"

"Yes. A flashlight might have attracted the attention of the club watchman. He's paid to watch the locker rooms and not the golf links, but a flashlight could have attracted his attention."

"That that's your story?"

"That's it."

"You're willing to stick to it?"

"Absolutely. It's the truth."

Mason regarded the man in thoughtful silence.

"Well?" Dutton asked, at length, squirming uncomfortably.

Mason said, "What about the gun?"

"What gun?"

"The gun you hid in the culvert."

Dutton's eyes widened.

"Go on," Mason said. "What about the gun you hid in the culvert?"

"You're crazy!"

Mason said, "Look, let's quit kidding each other and kidding ourselves. The police picked you up. They had enough evidence against you to contemplate charging you with murder.

"That can only mean one thing. They found the murder weapon and they traced it to you.

"You may not realize it, but the average amateur criminal always regards a culvert as a wonderful place to hide incriminating objects. They run true to form with devastating regularity.

"Therefore, when the police encounter a murder, one of the first things they do is to start looking in culverts on all roads leading away from the scene of the crime.

"Now, I'm willing to bet that you made a stop at a culvert, got out of your car and tossed the murder weapon and perhaps some other incriminating evidence into the culvert."

"And the police have *that*?" Dutton asked in dismay.

"The police have that."

"Then there's nothing left for *you* to do," Dutton said, "except have me plead guilty and put myself on the mercy of the court."

"Did you kill him?" Mason asked.

"No, I didn't kill him," Dutton said, "but I did find a gun by the body. I picked it up and when I got to my car, I examined it by flashlight and found it was my gun."

"You had a flashlight in the car?"

"Well, it was the dash light," Dutton said.

Mason said, "You're indulging in the most expensive luxury a man *can* indulge in."

"What's that? Being tried for murder?"

"No, lying to your lawyer."

"I'm not lying."

Mason said, "Don't be silly. A detective was watching you when you came out of the club. You jumped in your car and drove away at high speed. You went a mile and three-tenths, passed over a culvert, slammed on your brakes so you left tire marks on the surface of the pavement, put

80

your car in reverse; went back, got out and tossed something under the culvert. You didn't turn on the dash light; you didn't use any flashlight."

"A detective was watching me?"

"Yes."

"Then why wasn't I arrested?"

"It was a private detective and no one knew anything about the murder, as yet."

"All right," Dutton said. "You have me convicted in your own mind and—"

"I don't have you convicted in my mind," Mason said. "I simply suggested that you had better tell your lawyer the truth. How did you know it was your gun?"

"I looked at the gun on the ground."

"Then you must have had some light. What did you do, strike a match?"

"I had a small pocket flashlight in my coat. A very small, flat light which has a rechargeable battery. It gives a small field of illumination."

"Then you *did* have the means of looking around when you got out on the tee for the seventh hole?"

"Yes, I guess so, if I had used it."

"Why didn't you use it?"

"There wasn't any occasion to use it."

Mason said, "After you discovered the body, you did use it?"

"Yes."

"I was wondering," Mason said, "how you identified the body and how you identified the gun."

"Well, that was it. I had this flashlight with me."

"As soon as you recognized the gun as yours, you pocketed the gun and made a beeline for your car?"

"Yes."

Mason said, "I don't think you're that big a damn fool, Dutton. I think you're protecting someone."

"Protecting someone!" Dutton exclaimed.

"That's right."

"I'm trying to protect myself. I wish I could."

"Not with that story, you can't."

"Well, it's the only story I have."

Mason looked at his watch and said, "I have things to do. I'm going to tell you one thing. If you tell that story on the witness stand, you're going to be convicted."

"But why? The story is the truth."

"It may be the truth," Mason said, "but if that's so, it isn't all the truth. You're skipping over some incidents that might make your story convincing. You're trying to conceal things that you think might be against you. Hell, I don't know what you're doing, but every instinct I have as a lawyer tells me that once someone starts cross-examining you on that story, you're going to find yourself boxed in."

"No lawyer can cross-examine me and confuse me when I'm telling the truth," Dutton said.

"Exactly," Mason told him. "That's why I think you're going to be confused."

"Try it," Dutton invited. "Try cross-examining me."

"All right," Mason said, adopting a sneering, sarcastic attitude, "I'll pretend I'm the district attorney. Now, you answer questions. You're on the witness stand."

"Go right ahead," Dutton said.

"You had this flashlight in your pocket?" Mason said.

"Yes, sir."

"Why did you have it?"

"So I could—Well, I thought I might have to use it."

"For what purpose?"

"To identify the man I was to meet."

"You knew him?"

"I'd—Well, I talked with him over the telephone."

"Oh," Mason said, "you were going to use the flashlight then to identify his voice, is that right?"

"Well, I thought I'd take the flashlight along. It might come in handy."

"And it did come in very, very handy, didn't it?" Mason said sarcastically. "It enabled you to identify the body, to make sure he was very, very dead. It enabled you to search the body, to cut the labels off his clothes, to be certain you left nothing at all on the body so the corpse could readily be identified."

"I didn't say I had made sure he was dead."

"Well, then you didn't feel for a pulse?"

"No."

"In other words, the man might have been wounded and you simply took off for Ensenada on a vacation leaving a badly wounded man dying there on the golf course?"

"I could tell he was dead."

"How?"

"By—Well, he'd been shot."

"How did you know he'd been shot?"

"The gun was there."

"You found the gun with the aid of the flashlight?"

"Yes."

"And you knew it was your gun as soon as you saw it?"

"Yes."

"How? Did you check the numbers on the gun?"

"No, I . . . I recognized it."

"What was there about it that enabled you to recognize it?"

"The size, the shape."

"A thirty-eight-caliber Smith and Wesson short-barreled revolver?"

"Yes."

"Any distinguishing features about it?"

"Well . . . I just knew it was my gun, that's all."

"Certainly," Mason said, "you knew it was your gun because you had it in your pocket when you went out on the golf links. You knew it was your gun because you had loaded it and intended to murder the man who was trying to blackmail you. You knew it was your gun and you knew that you didn't dare to be caught with it in your possession. So you stopped your car in the middle of your flight and threw the gun under the culvert, hoping that it would remain there undiscovered."

Dutton cringed under Mason's sarcastic manner.

The lawyer got to his feet. "All right," he said. "That's a very weak sample of what you'll have to contend with. Hamilton Burger can be a demon when it comes to cross-examination.

"Think it over, Mr. Dutton.

"Whenever you're ready to change your story, send for me."

"What are you going to do?" Dutton asked. "Quit the case? Plead me guilty?"

"Are you guilty?" Mason asked.

"No."

"I never let a client plead guilty if he isn't guilty," Mason said. "I don't believe in it. I try to find the truth."

"You think I'm telling the truth?"

"No," Mason said, "but I still don't think you're a murderer. I think you're just a rotten liar. I hope you either improve by the time you get on the witness stand, or else have a different story to tell."

And with that, Mason signaled the officer who was waiting at the door of the conference room.

The lawyer walked out, and the barred door clanged shut.

Chapter 13

Desere Ellis said, "Oh, Mr. Mason, I'm so glad to see you. Isn't this simply too terrible for anything?"

Mason said, "These things nearly always look blacker at the start; then after the facts begin to come to light the case looks better. Are you willing to talk with me?"

"Willing? Why, I'm anxious! I've been wondering how I could get in touch with you. Tell me, how is the case against Kerry? Does it look bad? All I know is that he's been arrested."

"That," Mason said, "is something I can't tell you. I'm Kerry's attorney. I want you to understand that. I'm here as Kerry Dutton's lawyer. I'm representing him and no one else.

"Now, Dutton may be representing you, in a way, but that doesn't mean that *I'm* representing you. My whole interest in this case is to protect Kerry Dutton against the charges that have been made against him and to get an acquittal, if possible. Do you understand that?"

"Yes."

"All right," Mason said, "let's talk."

"Won't you be seated?" she asked, indicating a comfortable chair.

Mason said, "Thank you," and dropped into the chair.

"May I get you a drink?"

"No," Mason said, smiling, "I'm on duty and when I'm on duty I prefer not to drink. Now then, tell me about Dutton's gun."

"About . . . Dutton's . . . gun!"

"That's right."

Her eyes were wide with panic. "What about it?"

"Did he loan it to you?"

"Why . . . why, yes."

"Where is it?" Mason asked.

"In the drawer, in my bedroom."

"Let's go get it," Mason said.

"All right. I'll bring it to you."

"If it's all the same with you, I'd like to go with you," Mason said.

"Why?"

"One might say, to see how good an actress you are."

"What do you mean?" she flared.

"If you're telling the truth," Mason said, "I think I can detect it. If you're not, I think I can also tell that. It may make a big difference."

"In what way?"

"Let's get the gun first and then I'll tell you."

"All right," she said, "come with me."

She led the way down a passageway, opened the door of a typically feminine room, walked over to a dresser by the bed, triumphantly opened the drawer and then recoiled with her hand on her breast.

"It's . . . it's not here!"

"I didn't think it would be," Mason said dryly. "The gun was used in killing Rodger Palmer. Now, perhaps you'll tell me how *that* happened?"

"I don't know," she said. "I—I—Why, I just can't imagine. I would have sworn the gun was here."

Mason eyed her narrowly. "That," he said, "is exactly what I want you to do."

"What?"

"Swear that the gun was there."

"But . . . but what could have happened to it?"

"Someone took it," Mason said. "Unless you took it and used it."

"What do you mean?"

Mason said, "Did you, by any chance, go out to the Barclay Country Club the night of the murder?"

"No, why?"

"You are a member of the Barclay Club?"

"Yes."

"And, as such, have a key?"

"Heavens, I suppose so. There's one around here somewhere. Wait a minute, I had that in the drawer with the
gun."

"You say you *had* it?" Mason said. "That's past tense."

"All right, if you want to be technical about it, I *have* it."

"Let's take a look."

She rummaged through the back of the drawer and then
triumphantly produced a key.

"Now then," Mason said, "is there any chance that last
night you took this key and that gun, went out to the
Barclay Country Club, met Rodger Palmer on the seventh
tee, had an argument with him over blackmail and shot
him?"

"Good heavens, what are you talking about? Are you
crazy?"

"I don't think so," Mason said. "I'm just asking you if
that happened."

"No!"

Mason said, "There's a pretty good chance that the
Palmer murder was committed with Dutton's gun. Now
then, as far as you know, that gun was here in this drawer
until the day of the murder?"

She regarded him with white-faced emotion. "Of course
it was here. Only . . . only someone must have taken it, because it's gone."

"And you don't know when it was taken?"

Her forehead puckered into a contemplative frown. "I
saw it here two days ago, or was it three days ago. I was
cleaning out one of the other drawers and wanted a place
to put some things. I debated whether to put them in the
drawer with the gun. I remember I opened the drawer and
saw that the gun was there."

"And you haven't opened the drawer since then?"

"Heavens, Mr. Mason, I just don't know. I'm trying to
think. I come in here a dozen times a day. This is my bedroom. I keep things in the drawers. I open them and close
them. I—I'm only telling you what I can remember."

"All right," Mason said, "remember that the gun was

there two days ago; remember that you *thought* it was there when I asked you about it. You're going to have to swear to it."

"And this man, Palmer, was shot with Kerry's gun?"

"Apparently so. He was killed sometime during the night of the twenty-first."

"Can they . . . fix the time any more definitely than that it was just sometime during the night?"

"I think perhaps a little more definitely," Mason said, "but they *want* to fix it as being around sometime between nine-thirty and two-thirty, because that's when Kerry Dutton was out there at the golf club."

"He *was* out there?"

"Yes."

She was thoughtfully silent.

"Now then," Mason said, "is there any chance that Kerry Dutton could have been here in the house; could have gone into your bedroom and repossessed that gun from your bedroom drawer?"

She shook her head emphatically.

"Think it over," Mason said. "You see Kerry Dutton from time to time?"

"Mostly I talk with him over the telephone. He . . . he seems to avoid me."

"Has he been here within the last two days at any time that you can remember, prior to the time he had the fight?"

"No."

"You're sure?"

"Of course, I'm sure. He . . . he just wouldn't come near me. He was terribly hurt."

"Now, the night of the fight was the night of the murder. . . . Was he in your bedroom at any time prior to the start of the fight?"

"Not before the fight started, but afterwards they were all over the place."

"What happened?"

"Fred had been here to see me. He was elated. He wanted me to marry him and to use all the Steer Ridge Oil

88

stock to give him some money with which to carry out that pet project of his."

"What did you tell him?"

"I told him I'd have to think it over."

"Then what happened?"

"Then he went home and, shortly afterwards, Kerry was at the door."

"And what did Kerry want?"

"He said he wanted to talk with me privately."

"You invited him in?"

"Yes, of course."

"What was the situation between you? Were relations strained or cordial?"

"I tried to be cordial, but he was terribly standoffish. Finally I asked him what was the matter with him and why he had been so distant during the past few weeks, why he had been avoiding me.

"He said he had something to tell me, that it was going to be difficult. I thought he was going to tell me again how much he loved me and ask me to marry him."

"And you had told him prior to that time that the subject was distasteful to you, that you would be his young sister, but that if he wouldn't be content with that, you couldn't continue being friends?"

Her eyes shifted from Mason's, then she said suddenly, "I wish I'd bitten my tongue off before I'd told him that."

"Why? Had you changed your mind?"

"Frankly, Mr. Mason, I don't know. But it made such a difference in Kerry. It was just as if all the lights had gone off."

"All right, getting back to the night of the twenty-first," Mason said, "what happened? You asked him why he had been so distant?"

"Well, I . . . I was glad to see him but had the impression he'd been waiting outside watching Fred's car and waiting for Fred to drive away, and somehow there was something about that that I didn't like."

"And then what happened?"

"Fred had either forgotten something or else he knew

that Kerry was waiting. I don't know which. But Kerry was just telling me that he had something to tell me, that he hoped I wouldn't tell Fred or tell Fred's mother. He said they were trying to dominate my thinking and said I should quit running around with that type of person."

"And then," Mason prompted, as she hesitated.

"And then, all of a sudden, Fred's voice came from the doorway. He'd come back and hadn't knocked or pressed the button or anything. He just opened the door and stood there sneering."

"You said you heard his voice from the doorway?"

"Yes. He started telling Kerry a lot of things—that it was moneygrubbers like Kerry who were running the world, that really constructive thinkers stood no chance."

"Then what?"

"Then Kerry walked up to him, told him to shut up and get out, that he was talking to me and had some information that was for my ears alone."

"Go on," Mason said.

She said, "Fred's face got flushed with anger. Usually, he tries to appear to be cool, to hide his emotions beneath that attitude of calm contempt.

"This time, he got mad and said, 'Why, you little moneygrubbing pipsqueak,' and made a swing at Kerry."

"Did the blow land?"

She said, "I can't tell you everything that happened. I never saw anything in my life as fast as Kerry Dutton. He was all over the place, in and out, avoiding Fred's swings and punching Fred all over.

"Then Fred made a dash for the bedroom, and Kerry was right after him. Fred was screaming, and some woman in the adjoining apartment was shouting for the police. They were making a terrific noise; and in the bedroom some furniture got smashed."

"How did that happen?" Mason asked.

"They broke the nightstand, I guess, when someone fell against it; and someone jerked open a bureau drawer—not the upper one that had the gun, but one of the lower ones where I keep clothes and lingerie."

"And then?" Mason asked.

"Then Kerry really flattened him, because Fred was lying on the floor, and Kerry came running by me. He said, 'I'm sorry, Desere. I'll see you later.'

"I had already telephoned for the police while they were struggling in the bedroom. The woman in the adjoining apartment had been screaming for the police; and just a few minutes after Kerry left, and while Fred was getting himself together and trying to get to his feet, the police came and asked a lot of questions about what had happened.

"Fred told his story. But he lied, Mr. Mason. He lied about several things. My opinion of him went down when I heard the way he told the police what had happened."

"Did the police believe him?"

"At first, I think they did. Then they asked him to describe Kerry, and when he told them how tall he was and how much he weighed and how old he was and they looked at Fred Hedley standing over six feet, and broad-shouldered, one of the officers said to Fred, 'Well, you wouldn't have had any trouble if you'd landed that first punch.'

"And Fred walked right into the trap and said, 'You can say that again. The shifty little pipsqueak ducked that punch and slammed me in the stomach so hard it knocked the wind out of me. Then he was climbing all over me while I was half paralyzed from the solar plexus punch.'

"Then the officer grinned and said, 'So you really did start the fight? It was you that took the first punch.' "

"And then?" Mason asked.

"Then the officers told him he'd brought it on himself and refused to give him a warrant for Kerry's arrest."

Mason said, "Tell me a little more about what Hedley was talking about—what he wanted."

"What he wanted was an endowment for this art center of his."

"What is it—an art gallery, a school, or what?" Mason asked.

"Oh, it varies from time to time. It's one of his rather nebulous ideas. And yet, in some ways, it isn't so nebulous.

What he wants is to encourage artists to start a whole new school."

"A *new* school?"

"Well, more along the lines of a branch of modern art. Something that's a cross between the so-called modernistic school and the primitive school, interpretive art."

"He's quite definite in his ideas as to what he wants?"

"Well, as to *what* he wants, but not exactly how he intends to go about getting what he wants.

"Mainly he thinks that art is decadent; that color photography has made pictorial art, in the conventional sense, passé; that the so-called modernistic school is, at times, too lacking in the proper subject matter. So what he wants is to get people to paint things the way they see them, particularly portraits."

"He paints, himself?"

"Only vague outlines illustrating his technique."

"Do you have some of his paintings?"

"Not here, but—Well, he goes in for portraits. He encourages students to paint them with exaggerated facial characteristics.

"If you went to a conventional portrait painter, he'd smooth out all of your lines, and—Not that there *are* any lines, of course, I'm just talking figuratively—and soften the whole contour of the features so that you would be better looking.

"Hedley doesn't believe in that. He wants it done just the other way around. He emphasizes the predominant features. His paintings are something like colored cartoons. As he says, he paints the character rather than the flesh."

"And he wants you to endow that school of art?"

"Yes, to have it take its rightful place as the modern type of portrait painting."

"Do you think he could ever sell portraits of that sort?"

"Who knows? After the vogue catches on, he probably could. But that's why he needs to have an endowment, just to get started. You see, people probably wouldn't pose for their portraits—that is, not for that kind of a portrait . . . unless it became stylish."

"I can readily understand that much," Mason said.

She hurried on. "His first subjects would be prominent men that he'd get from the newspapers. You see very good pen-and-ink, black-and-white cartoons, but what he wants to do is to make something that is almost a cartoon— not quite. It stops just short of being a cartoon but it would be in color and would be beautifully done."

"Does he have the ability and technique to do it beautifully?"

"Not now. He wants to develop. Really, Mr. Mason, I don't know why you started cross-examining me about Fred Hedley."

"Because I'm trying to get certain facts and I want to have those facts straight. Now, when Hedley talks about an endowment, he really means he wants to give financial aid to certain aspiring artists who can't make a living otherwise. Is that right?"

"I guess so, yes."

"And *he's* an aspiring artist who can't make a living?"

"He *may* be the founder of a whole new school of painting."

"And he intends to subsidize himself?"

"He says he'd be untrue to his art if he didn't."

"With *your* money?"

"Of course. What other money would he have?"

"That's a good question," Mason said.

"Well, of course, he despises moneygrubbing."

"All right," Mason said, "the police are going to question you."

"But I can't understand how anything like that could have happened. I mean, how Kerry could have taken the gun."

"He had plenty of opportunity," Mason said, "but if we're going to save Dutton's neck, we've got to find out *how* it happened. Unless, of course, Dutton killed him."

"Do you think he did, Mr. Mason?"

"He's my client," Mason said with a wry smile. And then after a moment, "Thank you very much for your co-operation, Miss Ellis."

Chapter 14

Paul Drake sat in Mason's office with a notebook balanced on his knee and said, "Our men have uncovered a lot of stuff. None of it is going to help."

"Go on," Mason said, "give me the facts."

"Well, Rodger Palmer was a great believer in the Steer Ridge Oil stock, but he hated Jarvis Reader, the head of the company.

"I don't know whether you noticed it or not, Perry, but there's a lot of similarity in the appearance of the two men. Reader is perhaps a few years younger, but both men were two-fisted oil men who had worked as roughnecks, who believed in direct action but who had ideas that were diametrically opposed.

"Palmer believed in developing a company working along proven structures, taking a chance on wildcatting after scientific exploration of the structures indicated there was a reasonable chance.

"Jarvis Reader is a plunger. He wants to be a big shot, the bigger the better. He made his money, not by operating oil wells but by selling stock, paying himself a fancy salary and making his reports to the stockholders look good by tying up huge blocks of acreage.

"Now, of course, you can't tie up acreage like that in really good oil country, and the Steer Ridge Oil Company was going steadily downhill until it had that lucky strike.

"Reader is a flashy dresser, a big spender, regards himself as the big executive type, has a twin-motored airplane at his beck and call and is *always* the big shot.

"After Rodger Palmer got out of the company, he had periods of pretty lean living. He hung around cheap hotels. Sometimes he would be in rooming houses where shady characters lived. Once he was even questioned by the police in connection with the nylon stocking strangling of a prostitute. He had been in the rooming house at the time, but fortunately had an alibi. He had been talking with the clerk at the time the actual murder must have been committed.

"But that gives you a general idea of the guy's background. His clothes were seedy, he was pretty much discredited in the oil game.

"Then he started calling on stockholders in the Steer Ridge Company, telling them that they were being bilked, and he put up a pretty convincing argument. I understand a group of stockholders, who controlled a large block of the stock, gave him money to try and get proxies so that Reader could be ousted.

"Now then, you asked about Fred Hedley the night of the murder and whether he could possibly have been out there at the country club at the time the murder was committed.

"There's not a chance. At the time the murder must have been committed, Hedley was in a drugstore having his face patched. After that fight he was out of circulation and pretty badly messed up.

"He found an all-night drugstore, and the clerk helped him put on disinfectants and patched him up."

"All right," Mason said, with a sigh. "We go to trial tomorrow and, so far, every single thing we've uncovered not only hasn't helped us but is ammunition the district attorney can use."

"And he'll sure use it," Drake said. "He'd rather win this case than any case he's ever tried. The way he looks at it, he's running downhill all the way."

Mason said, "It looks that way, Paul, but we'll give him a fight for every inch of ground we have to hold."

Chapter 15

Judge Eduardo Alvarado opened the second day of the trial by saying, "Gentlemen, I hope we can get a jury today."

"I see no reason why we can't," Perry Mason said.

"The peremptory is with the prosecution," Judge Alvarado said.

"The prosecution passes."

Mason arose, bowed and smiled. "Let the jury be sworn," he said. "The defense has no further peremptories and is satisfied with this jury."

Judge Alvarado smiled as he said, "Well, I hardly expected such prompt action. I thank you, gentlemen. The clerk will now swear the jury and then Court will take a ten-minute recess."

At the conclusion of the recess, Judge Alvarado nodded to the table of the prosecution where Stevenson Bailey, one of the trial deputies, sat next to Hamilton Burger, the district attorney.

"Make your opening speech, Mr. Prosecutor," the judge said.

Bailey said, "If it please the Court, and you members of the jury, this is going to be perhaps the briefest opening statement I have ever made.

"For the most part I am going to let the facts speak for themselves, but because they are somewhat complicated I will give you a brief outline.

"The defendant, Kerry Dutton, was trustee under a so-called spendthrift trust created by Templeton Ellis in favor of his daughter, Desere Ellis.

"Under the terms of this trust, the defendant, Dutton, had the right to sell securities as he saw fit, purchase other securities, and to pay out such money as he saw fit to the beneficiary of the trust.

"Now then, ladies and gentlemen, we expect to prove that in the three years and some months, almost four years, during which this trust had been in effect—" And here Bailey held up four fingers in front of the jury—"during all of those four years, the defendant in this case *never made a single accounting to the beneficiary of the trust.*"

Bailey paused to let that statement sink in.

"Furthermore, ladies and gentlemen of the jury, we propose to show that the defendant, Dutton, had systematically looted that trust, using income from it to feather his own financial nest until he had built up an independent fortune in his own name through shrewd investments and manipulations but *he never—made—an—accounting!*"

Again there was a moment of silence.

"As a part of the holdings of the trust, there had been stock in the Steer Ridge Oil and Refining Company. This stock was highly speculative. At one time it was rather high; then it went to a low where the value was only nominal; and then when oil had been struck, the property skyrocketed.

"We expect to show that Rodger Palmer, the decedent, had known the executive officials of the Steer Ridge Oil and Refining Company for some time, had also known Templeton Ellis, the father of Desere Ellis.

"We expect to show that Rodger Palmer wanted the defendant to give him a proxy enabling the decedent to vote the trust stock in the Steer Ridge Company. The defendant refused, because he had to refuse, since he had sold the Steer Ridge stock. The decedent didn't know of this sale, but we can show by inference at least that he did know of a purchase of a large block of Steer Ridge stock the defendant had made in his own name.

"The decedent, Rodger Palmer, was threatening the defendant with exposure unless he received a proxy and the sum of five thousand dollars with which to carry on his proxy fight.

"Now, we expect to show this and to show that Rodger

Palmer made a final appointment with the defendant at approximately ten o'clock on the night of the twenty-first of September.

"I say that it was a final appointment, because the defendant kept that appointment and, at that time, killed Rodger Palmer. The decedent, Rodger Palmer, had demanded five thousand dollars as the price of his silence. The defendant had been prepared to pay that price if he had to. He had drawn five thousand dollars from his bank and had the money on him in cash when he was apprehended.

"But the defendant knew that blackmail was endless. The blackmailer's attitude would be even more eager, his appetite the more voracious by receiving this payment.

"So after due consideration, after careful deliberation, Kerry Dutton decided on murder as his best way out.

"The murder, ladies and gentlemen, took place at the seventh tee of the exclusive Barclay Country Club. The body was not found until the next morning.

"By that time the defendant had fled to Mexico and was registered at an auto court under the name of Frank Kerry.

"We may never know all the information Palmer was holding over the defendant's head. We can surmise some of it. The circumstantial evidence screams to heaven of blackmail.

"We further propose to show that along the path of his flight, the defendant paused long enough to throw the gun, the murder weapon with which Rodger Palmer was killed, under a culvert.

"On the strength of that evidence, ladies and gentlemen of the jury, we expect to ask for a verdict of first-degree murder.

"We thank you."

Bailey bowed with courtly dignity, strode back to the counsel table, and sat down.

"Do you wish to make an opening statement at this time?" Judge Alvarado asked Perry Mason.

"We will defer our opening statement until the defense is ready to put on its case," Mason said.

"Very well," Judge Alvarado said, "call your first witness, Mr. Prosecutor."

Bailey called the autopsy surgeon who testified to having performed an autopsy on the body of Rodger Palmer. The death had been caused by a single gunshot wound in the head, which had been fired into the right temple from a gun which had been not more than six inches away from the man's head at the time of its discharge.

Asked as to the time of death, he fixed the time of death as between nine-thirty o'clock and two-thirty A.M. on the night of the twenty-first and twenty-second of September.

"Cross-examine," Bailey snapped at Mason.

Mason said, almost casually, "Death could have been at nine o'clock, Doctor?"

"I doubt it."

"At eight-thirty?"

"I don't think so."

"But it *could* have been at eight-thirty?"

"It's possible but not probable. I fix nine-thirty as the earliest hour."

"But it's *possible* death occurred at eight-thirty?"

"But not probable. You can't fix the time of death with a stopwatch."

"That's all, Doctor, thank you."

In rapid succession, Bailey called witnesses who testified to Rodger Palmer's interest in the Steer Ridge Oil and Refining Company, to his friendship with Templeton Ellis, and to the fact that he had, shortly prior to his death, been engaged in a quiet campaign to secure proxies in the Steer Ridge Oil and Refining Company in his name.

Mason brushed all of these witnesses aside with the casual comment, "No questions," when he was asked to cross-examine.

Judge Alvarado watched the lawyer with thoughtful curiosity as it became apparent Mason did not intend to engage in routine cross-examination.

"Call Miss Desere Ellis to the stand," Bailey said, in the manner of one making a dramatic announcement.

Desere Ellis came forward, her manner subdued, her eyes purposely avoiding those of Kerry Dutton.

She took the oath, seated herself on the stand, and faced the prosecutor with the manner of a courageous woman who is facing an ordeal and is determined to be brave.

Under skillful questioning by Bailey she told about her father's death, the reading of the will, the initial conversations with the defendant about the trust.

"Now then," Bailey said, "when did the defendant make his first accounting under the trust?"

"He never made any accounting."

"Never—made—any—accounting?" Bailey repeated.

"No, sir, no *formal* accounting."

"Well, were there any other accountings, any *informal* accountings?"

"Well, he discussed, from time to time, the securities which he had sold in order to give me my allowance."

"And did he make any comments at that time in regard to the principal of the trust?"

"He said at one time that he had sold nearly all of the securities which my father had left."

"Thereby giving you the impression that there would be no funds available to you after the termination of the trust?"

"I had that impression, yes."

"Did the defendant, at any time, tell you that there was a large sum of money in the trust which he would have to pay over to you or to which you would be entitled on the termination of the trust period?"

She shifted her position on the witness stand, started to glance at Dutton, then lowered her eyes.

"No," she said.

"Did he ever tell you he had sold your Steer Ridge stock at a dollar a share, then, later on, purchased a similar block of Steer Ridge stock *in his own name* at from ten to fifteen cents a share?"

"No."

"Did he tell you he had made this purchase only a few days before the stock had skyrocketed in value?"

"No."

"Did he tell you he had secured inside information that Steer Ridge was drilling in a most promising formation?"

"No."

"Did you have any reason to believe your Steer Ridge stock had been sold?"

"No."

"The defendant never told you so?"

"No."

Bailey said to Perry Mason, "Cross-examine."

Mason arose and approached the witness, his manner courteous, pausing when he was some five steps from the witness stand, waiting until she raised her eyes to his.

Mason said in a kindly voice, "You had the impression that your trust funds would be exhausted when the time came to terminate the trust?"

"Yes."

"That was an impression you had in your mind?"

"Yes."

"Now then," Mason said, holding up his left index finger, "please follow this question very closely. Are you prepared to do so?"

"Yes, sir," she said, her eyes on his finger.

Mason moved the finger, slowly, beating time to the words, "Did you get this impression from your own thinking, or *did the defendant ever tell you in so many words that the trust fund would be exhausted at the time the trust terminated?*"

"I . . . I had that impression."

"I know you did," Mason said, "and it is quite possible that the defendant knew you did, but I am asking now if the defendant ever *told you in so many words* definitely, positively, that the trust fund would be exhausted at the time the trust terminated?"

"I can't remember his ever having said that."

"That's all," Mason said.

"Just one more question on redirect," Bailey said. "Did the defendant ever tell you in so many words, Miss Ellis, that there would be a large sum of money coming to you on the termination of your trust?"

"No, sir," she said, promptly.

"That's all," Bailey said.

"Just one more question on recross?" Mason asked. "Miss Ellis, did you ever ask the defendant?"

"No, I can't remember doing that."

"In other words, you took the situation for granted?"

"Yes."

"That's all," Mason said.

Bailey was again on his feet, "I'm going to ask one more question on redirect. Isn't it a fact that the defendant was fully aware of your feeling that the trust fund would be exhausted?"

"Objected to," Mason said, "as calling for a conclusion of the witness."

"All right, all right, if I have to do it the long way around, I'll do it the long way around," Bailey said in exasperation. "Isn't it a fact that the defendant let you know by his own words that he understood you felt the termination of the trust would leave you with no funds?"

"Objected to as calling for a conclusion of the witness and on the further ground that it is leading and suggestive."

"It's redirect examination," Bailey said.

"I don't care what it is," Mason said. "A man has no more right to lead his witness on redirect than he does on direct. Furthermore, this calls for a conclusion of the witness as to what the defendant said. Let's have a question calling for the defendant's exact words."

Bailey waved his hands in a gesture of dismissal. "I think the jury understands the situation. I'm not going to bicker with counsel. That's all, Miss Ellis."

Mason smiled. "*That's* all."

"I'll call Mrs. Rosanna Hedley to the stand," Bailey said.

Mrs. Hedley assumed her position on the witness stand with a very visible chip on her shoulder. She didn't intend to be confused by any attorney.

"Did you ever hear a conversation between Desere Ellis and the defendant in which she asked him about the condition of the trust funds?" Bailey asked.

"Yes, sir."

"Do you remember when that was?"

"I remember exactly when it was. That was on the fourth day of July, on the evening of the fourth of July."

"Who was present?"

"My son was present, that is, he had been present."

"And by your son, you mean Fred Hedley?"

"That's right," she said. "Fred Hedley, the artist."

Bailey smiled almost imperceptibly. "Exactly," he said. "Was Fred there at the time of this conversation?"

"No, he had left the room."

"Then who was present?"

"Just Miss Ellis, the defendant, and myself."

"And what did Miss Ellis say?"

"She asked the defendant how the trust was coming what she could count on."

"And what did the defendant say in response to the question?"

"He told her that he thought the trust funds would last out the duration of the trust, letting her have the same allowance she'd been having."

"Move to strike the answer," Mason said, "as not being responsive to the question and as being a conclusion of the witness. The witness should state the exact words used by the defendant as nearly as she can recollect."

"The motion is granted. The answer will go out. The witness will answer the question as to exactly what the defendant said."

"You mean I have to give his exact words?" Mrs. Hedley asked.

"As nearly as you can," Judge Alvarado explained, not unkindly. "When you give your impression of his words, you are not giving the exact words but a conclusion you drew from the conversation. Can you remember exactly what he said?"

"Well, as nearly as I can remember, he said, with one of those oily smiles, 'Don't worry, Desere, there will be money enough in the trust fund to keep your allowance until the trust expires.' "

"Cross-examine," Bailey snapped.

Mason smiled. "His smile was oily, Mrs. Hedley?"

"Oily," she repeated.

"What do you mean by an oily smile?" Mason asked.

"You know what I mean, a smirk, a simper."

"Greasy?" Mason asked.

"Oily!" she snapped.

"That gives a pretty good picture of your feeling for the defendant, does it not?" Mason asked.

"A feeling which events have amply justified," she said acidly.

"Now then," Mason said, "he told her there would be enough money to last out the trust?"

"Yes."

"In other words," Mason said, "he was predicting the future. We might have had another crash in the security market."

"Yes," she said, "the world might have come to an end."

"And there *was* enough money in the trust to carry through Desere's allowance to the end of the trust, was there not?" Mason said.

"That much and nearly two hundred and fifty thousand more."

"Then he didn't lie to her, did he?"

"He deceived her."

"But he didn't lie to her."

"Objected to as argumentative, as calling for a conclusion of the witness," Bailey said. "If the defense is going to be technical, *I'll* be technical."

Mason smiled blandly and said, "I'll withdraw the question. I think the jury has the picture in mind," and sat down.

Bailey called a ballistics expert, who identified the Smith & Wesson revolver introduced in evidence as the murder weapon. He then called a firearms dealer who identified the gun as having been sold by him to the defendant, and introduced in evidence the certificate of purchase, bearing the signature of the defendant.

Bailey also introduced maps showing the scene of the murder; photographs of the terrain; of the body, and of the clothes worn by the decedent. He introduced the coat worn by Palmer when the body was discovered and called attention to the fact that the labels had been cut from the garment.

The coroner testified there were no keys, no money, no handkerchief, no knife, nothing in the pockets.

Bailey called Lt. Tragg to the stand. Tragg testified to having been advised of the murder, going to the golf club, inspecting the body and the premises; then looking in the culverts along the road leading from the golf club.

"Why did you do this?" Bailey asked.

"It's a routine police procedure."

"What did you find, if anything?"

"I found this gun, tagged People's Exhibit A-G, in a culvert, one and three-tenths miles from the entrance to the golf club."

"And what did you do with that gun?"

"I traced the registration on it."

"How long did that take you?"

"Only a few minutes after it was found. We ran down the serial number."

"What else did you do, if anything?"

"When we connected the serial number with the defendant, we got the license number of his automobile and put out an all-points bulletin."

"And did that all-points bulletin include certain cities in Mexico?"

"We have an arrangement on important homicide cases by which the Mexican police in Ensenada, Tijuana and Mexicali co-operate with us."

"And what did you find?"

"We found the defendant registered in Ensenada—"

"Just a moment," Mason interrupted. "Is the witness testifying as to what he found or what the Mexican police found? In the latter event, it is hearsay."

"Quite right," Bailey said. "Don't testify to anything you have been told, Lieutenant Tragg."

"Well, then I can't testify to his being in Mexico," Lt. Tragg said with a smile.

"Where did you, personally, find the defendant?"

"At the international border, just outside of Tecate," Tragg said.

"And how did you happen to find him there?"

"The Mexican police pushed him across the line."

"And what did you do?"

"Took him in custody."

"Did you have any conversation with the defendant at that time?"

"Yes."

"Did you tell him that he was accused of murder?"

"I told him that he was wanted for questioning in connection with the murder of Rodger Palmer."

"Did you ask him where he had been at the time the murder was committed or approximately that time?"

"I asked him many questions, and his answer was the same to all of them."

"What was his answer?"

" 'I refuse to make any statement until I have consulted my attorney!' "

"That was his answer to all questions?"

"Well, I asked him why, if he had nothing to conceal, he had registered under the name of Frank Kerry in Mexico, and he stated that actually Kerry was his middle name, that Frank was his first name and his full name was Frank Kerry Dutton."

"I see," Bailey said. "Cross-examine."

"Why, no questions at all," Mason said, with a gesture of his hand.

There was a note of triumph in Bailey's voice as he said, "Call Thomas Densmore Fulton to the stand."

Fulton came forward and was sworn.

"What is your occupation?"

"I am a private detective."

"By whom are you employed?"

"Mostly by the Drake Detective Agency."

"On the twenty-first day of September last, by whom were you employed?"

"Paul Drake."

"What were your instructions?"

"To shadow a subject."

"Who was the subject?"

"The defendant, Kerry Dutton."

"And in connection with your duties, did you follow Kerry Dutton anywhere?"

"I did. Yes, sir."

"Where?"

"I followed him to a telephone booth."

"Where was that telephone booth?"

"At a service station on the corner of Figueroa and Boulevard Way."

"Was the service station open or closed?"

"The service station was closed. It was a big service station with quite a bit of parking space, but the telephone booth was open."

"What did you do?"

"I saw the defendant enter the telephone booth and I drove my car from across the street and into the parking station. He dialed a number, then hung up the phone and after a short interval, dialed again. I ran up to the booth as though I were in a hurry to use the telephone."

"What did the defendant do?"

"He motioned me away."

"What did you do?"

"I surreptitiously planted a wire recorder with a rubber suction cup so that the microphone, which is very sensitive, would pick up sounds within the booth."

"Then what did you do?"

"Returned to my car."

"And what happened after that?"

"The defendant emerged from the telephone booth, jumped in his car and took off."

"What did you do?"

"I tried to follow him."

"Were you able to do so?"

"No, sir."

"Why?"

"The defendant drove like crazy. He went through three

or four red lights, through a boulevard stop, nearly had a collision with another car, left me stymied in cross-traffic and got away."

"So, what did you do?"

"I returned to the telephone booth to pick up the wire recorder and see if I had a clue there."

"And you picked up the wire recorder?"

"Yes, sir."

"Then what did you do?"

"I rewound the wire to the starting position and turned the key over to listening and listened to the recording."

"Do you have that wire recorder here?"

"I do."

"If the Court please," Bailey said, "I believe the conversation on the wire recorder is the best evidence. It is not as clear as I would like to have it, but it is, nevertheless, understandable. I have arranged for an amplifier and I would like to have this conversation played directly to the jury."

"No objection," Mason said.

Rather dramatically, Bailey set up the wire recorder, in connection with the amplifier, and turned on the current. A buzzing sound filled the courtroom, then the sound of a man's voice. "Hello, what's new? You know who this is."

There was a brief interval of silence, then the voice said, "I called this other number for instructions; I was told to call you here at this pay station. . . . Yes, I have the five thousand and will pay it over if things are as you represented—if you're acting in good faith."

There was an interval of silence; then the man's voice said, "Give me that place again. The seventh tee at the Barclay Country Club . . . why in the world pick that sort of a place? . . . When? . . . Good heavens, it's nearly that time now . . . All right. All right! I'll get out there. Yes, I've got a key to the club. I'll be there."

There was an abrupt click as the recording ended.

"That, if the Court and the jury please," Bailey said, "is the termination of the conversation."

Bailey turned to the witness. "What did you do after hearing that conversation?"

"I went at once to the Barclay Country Club."

"What did you find there?"

"I found the defendant's automobile parked there."

"How long did it take you to get there from the time you listened to that conversation on the tape recorder?"

"Probably fifteen minutes."

"And what did you do?"

"I tried the door of the club, but it was locked. I waited until the defendant came out."

"How long was that?"

"I arrived at ten-ten. The defendant emerged at ten-twenty-two."

"Now, let's get this time element straight," Bailey said. "You tried to follow the defendant?"

"That's right."

"He was driving, as you said, like crazy. He went through red lights and boulevard stops?"

"Three red lights; one boulevard stop."

"You lost him?"

"That's right."

"You returned to the telephone booth?"

"Yes, sir."

"You picked up your recording device and listened to the conversation?"

"Yes, sir."

"How long, in your opinion, was that from the time you had left the telephone booth following the defendant?"

"Probably five minutes."

"And then you went directly to the Barclay Country Club?"

"Yes."

"And you waited at the Barclay Country Club for how long?"

"Eleven minutes . . . nearly twelve minutes."

"And then the defendant came out?"

"Yes, sir."

"And what did he do?"

"He drove down the road for a mile and three-tenths."

"And then what?"

"Then he brought his car to an abrupt stop and started backing up."

"What did you do?"

"I had to drive on past him so he wouldn't be suspicious."

"And then what?"

"I went half a mile down the road, jumped out of the car, put a bumper jack under the rear bumper and acted as if I had a flat tire."

"And what happened?"

"Within a matter of seconds the defendant's car went past me again, going at high speed."

"What did you do?"

"I hurriedly removed the bumper jack, tossed it in the back of the car, and stepped on the throttle."

"And were you able to follow the defendant?"

"Yes, sir."

"How far did you follow him?"

"To Ensenada."

"Where in Ensenada?"

"To the Siesta del Tarde Auto Court."

"And then what did you do?"

"I telephoned Paul Drake that the subject was registered at the Siesta del Tarde Auto Court under the name of Frank Kerry."

"And then what?"

"Then Perry Mason and his secretary, Della Street, showed up and I told them where the defendant was and they went to his room."

"Then what?"

"Then the Mexican police came."

Bailey smiled. "Cross-examine," he said to Mason.

Mason said, "Your wire recording gives only one side of the conversation?"

"That's right."

"You don't know whom the defendant was calling?"

"No, sir."

"You don't know what words were used on the other end of the line?"

"No, sir."

"That's all," Mason said.

Judge Alvarado said, "It is now time for the evening adjournment. I congratulate counsel for both sides on the speed with which this trial is progressing.

"During the evening the jurors will not converse among themselves or with anyone else about the case, nor will they read newspaper accounts of the trial or listen to anything on radio or television pertaining to the trial. They will avoid forming or expressing any opinion until the case is finally submitted for a decision. If anyone should approach any of you jurors to discuss the case, report that matter to the Court.

"Court will take a recess until ten o'clock tomorrow morning."

Chapter 16

Mason sat in the visiting room of the jail and let his eyes bore into those of his client.

"This," he said, "is your last chance."

"I'm telling you the truth."

"You can't ever change your story from this point on," Mason warned. "If you ever get on the witness stand, tell your story and then are forced to change it under cross-examination, you're a gone goose."

Dutton nodded.

"And don't discount Hamilton Burger's ability as a cross-examiner."

"Do you think I'm going to have to get on the stand?"

"You're going to have to get on the stand," Mason said. "They have a dead open-and-shut case against you. You're not only going to have to get on the stand, but you are going to have to persuade the jury that you're telling the truth.

"Now then, if they catch you in some little lie—just anything—the time you get up in the morning, how many lumps of sugar you had in your coffee, just anything that is false, they're going to hold it against you all the way down the line."

"I've told you the truth," Dutton said.

"You aren't trying to protect someone? You aren't shading the facts in order to make it easy on Desere Ellis?"

He shook his head.

"And you aren't trying to protect yourself?"

"No, I've told you the truth."

"Palmer had given you a number to call on the dot at nine-forty-five?"

Dutton nodded.

"You went to the telephone booth, called this number

and were given another number, both numbers were pay stations, a voice told you to meet Palmer at the seventh tee at the Barclay Country Club when you called the second number?"

"Right."

"Now, was that last voice a woman's?"

"I don't know. At the time I thought it was a man trying to talk in a high-pitched voice so as to disguise it; now I just don't know. All I know is it was high-pitched for a man's voice, low-pitched for a woman's."

"What was the number you called?"

"It was a phone booth. I've forgotten the number. Palmer told me that he'd have someone there to take the call and tell me where he could meet me; that it would be a pay station I was calling so not to try to do anything funny."

"Now then, you remained in the phone booth and called a number?"

"Right."

"That was the number of a pay station?"

"That's right."

"And what happened when you called that number?"

"A voice answered, said, 'Take a pencil, write down this number and call it in exactly ten seconds—no more, no less.' I feel sure that first voice was a man's voice— Well, I'm not absolutely certain. It was sort of disguised."

"And you wrote down the number?"

"Yes."

"What was the idea of the two numbers?"

"Apparently so I couldn't locate the number in time to have police or private detectives get on the job and find out where I was to meet Palmer or in time to set up recording devices so they could catch him."

"But if you knew that it was Palmer you were going to be meeting . . ."

"I knew it was Palmer. I also knew he was supposed to have evidence that was going to discredit Fred Hedley."

"And why did you want that evidence?"

"You know why."

"I'm asking you so I can hear it in your words just the way you'll be telling it to a jury."

"I wanted to protect Desere Ellis."

"Why?"

"Because ... well, because that was my job under the will."

"Whom were you protecting her from?"

"From herself, largely; and also from a man who was trying to take advantage of her."

Mason regarded his client thoughtfully, abruptly got to his feet. "All right, Dutton, I don't want you to think I'm rehearsing you. I don't want you to rehearse yourself. I don't want you to get on that witness stand and act as if your story had been rehearsed. I want you to tell the truth and it had better look as if you're telling the truth."

"I'll do my best, Mr. Mason," Dutton said.

Mason nodded. "Get some sleep. It's going to be an ordeal, and don't think it won't be."

Chapter 17

When Perry Mason returned to his office, Della Street said, "Paul Drake has a witness, Chief."

"Where is he?"

"They're in Paul's office."

"Who's the witness?"

"A man who lives within about a hundred yards of the fairway at the Barclay Country Club. His house is not too far from the tee-off position on hole number seven.

"He heard a shot on the night of the twenty-first and it was earlier than the time the prosecution thinks the murder was committed."

Perry Mason's face lit up in a smile. "I've been waiting for a break in this case," he said, "and this may be it. Get him in here, Della."

Della manipulated the dial of the phone and a moment later she said, "He's on his way."

"Now then," Mason said, "get me a blank subpoena on behalf of the defense. As soon as I ask this fellow his name, you take it down, slip out to the other office, fill the name in on the subpoena and return it to me.

"No matter what happens we aren't going to let this man leave this office without having a subpoena slapped on him as a defense witness."

Della Street nodded, moved over to the filing case, took out the folder in the case of People of the State of California vs. Kerry Dutton, removed the original subpoena and a copy; then stepped out to the other office to place them out of sight.

"All ready," she said.

Drake's code knock sounded on the exit door.

Mason nodded to Della Street, who opened the door.

Paul Drake ushered in a tall, somewhat loose-jointed man in his middle fifties; a man with keen eyes, bushy eyebrows, prominent ears, a long thin neck.

"This is Mr. Mason," Drake said. "Mason, this is George Holbrook. Mr. Holbrook lives out by the Barclay Country Club."

"George Holbrook, is it?" Mason asked, shaking hands. "Any middle initial, Mr. Holbrook?"

"Sure," Holbrook said, grinning. "A conventional one. George W. Holbrook. The 'W' standing for Washington."

Della Street silently slipped from the room.

"Well, sit down, Mr. Holbrook," Mason said. "I understand you know something about this case?"

"Maybe I do and maybe I don't," Holbrook said, sitting down in the chair and crossing his long legs in front of him, then after a moment clasping bony fingers around his upthrust right knee.

"Trouble is, Mr. Mason, you can't tell these days what you hear. There are so many sounds, so many noises, among them sonic booms, a fellow never knows quite what he *does* hear."

"Suppose you tell me about it," Mason said.

"Well, I got to reading about this thing in the paper and all of a sudden it struck me right between the eyes. I said to my wife, 'Hey, wait a minute, wasn't that the night I heard the shot?' "

"You're not certain of the date?" Mason asked, his voice showing his disappointment.

"Now, wait a minute," Holbrook said. "I *think* I can fix the date all right. I was telling you what I'd said to the wife."

"Go ahead," Mason said.

"We'd just got a wire from my wife's sister that she was arriving on the ten-fifty plane and we were sitting there talking it over. Then my wife went out in the kitchen and I stepped out on the front porch for a little breath of air—and a puff or two on a cigarette."

Holbrook grinned. "The wife doesn't like smoking in the house. She has a very sensitive nose, and tobacco smell just doesn't agree with her, so I kind of step out when I'm smoking and— Well, she'd like to have me swear off. I guess she thinks I have. So what with one thing and another, I kind of sneak out when I'm smoking."

"Go ahead," Mason said.

"Well, I heard this shot. I'm pretty darn sure it was a shot. I've done hunting in my time and I think I know a shot when I hear one."

"And what happened?"

"Well, I stood there looking, trying to see where the shot came from."

"You couldn't locate it from the sound?"

"I think it was out on the golf course somewhere. That's where it sounded like."

"You checked the date because of the arrival of your sister?"

"That's right. She came on the twenty-first."

"How did it happen," Mason said, "that the next morning, with the papers full of a body having been found on the golf course, you didn't connect up the shot with the murder?"

"That was simple," Holbrook said. "The wife's sister had always wanted to take a motor tour and she was due in at ten-fifty. We picked her up at the airport and, of course, she was all packed, so my wife suggested we take the motor trip she'd been wanting. I guess the women had had it planned that way all along. They'd been using the long distance phone back and forth. You can't get ahead of a couple of women—can't get ahead of one, for that matter.

"Well, anyway we started off at six o'clock the next morning, had breakfast along the road, and took a swing up through Northern California around the Redwood Highway, then came back through Yosemite Park. What's more, with the excitement of the sister coming, and going down and meeting the plane and all that, I just pretty nearly forgot about that shot. It wasn't until I got to reading in the paper about this case that I got to thinking about it again."

"You hadn't heard about the murder?" Mason asked.

"Why, sure we'd heard about it," Holbrook said. "Talked about it, as a matter of fact.

"I first heard it on the radio when we were between Modesto and Sacramento, somewhere along in there. I didn't pay too much attention to it the first time I heard it, just a murder that had been committed on a golf course. Then the second time, my wife perked up and said, 'Why George, that's the golf course near our house.' And I got to thinking and said, 'I guess that's where it was all right.'

"Then we got to Sacramento and stayed there overnight. Then went on up to Redding and I got a San Francisco paper in Redding and— Well, I just sort of like to keep in touch with the comic strips."

Holbrook broke off to grin amiably at Mason. "Wife says I'm just a grown-up juvenile; but doggone it, I *do* like to read the comic strips."

Mason nodded.

"Well, there was something in the paper there about the body being found on the seventh tee. I didn't pay much attention to what that meant because, until a few days ago, I didn't know where the seventh tee was. I'm retired and the income isn't enough to afford golf.

"It was after this trial started that one of the newspapers published a map of the golf course. That's a long course. It stretches down quite a ways and has about six holes strung out one right after the other."

"And this map showed the location of the body?"

"That's right. Showed it with reference to the seventh tee and showed the seventh tee with reference to the streets— the cross streets out there."

Holbrook shifted his position. "You see, when the golf course was first laid out, that was all open land out there but they only owned just so much of it so they kept the golf course on the land they owned. Then with the golf course there, the subdividers moved in and it seems like in no time at all the thing was all built up.

"We bought our house right after the big boom—and that was fifteen years ago, I guess. I was working then. Been living there ever since."

"Have you ever played golf?"

"Got no use for it. As far as I'm concerned, it's just taking a bunch of sticks, going up to a ball, hitting the ball where the sticks aren't, then packing the sticks up to where the ball is and repeating it all over."

Mason said, "Can you fix the exact time that you heard the shot?"

"Now, that's what I'm talking about," Holbrook said. "I'm really certain that it was way before ten o'clock."

"How do you know?"

"Because I listen to news at ten o'clock and I'm pretty sure the news hadn't come on yet."

"How long before ten o'clock?"

"Well, I was out there on the porch taking a smoke and—"

"Was it dark?" Mason asked.

"Yes, it was dark. I remember the cigarette glowed when I threw it away out there on the front lawn, and I got to wondering if my wife had maybe seen the end of the cigarette glowing when I threw it—but she hadn't. That doesn't mean she didn't know what I went out there for, but I guess she was excited over her sister coming and all.

"And all of a sudden, I realized it was time for that ten o'clock news I like to listen to on TV. I was just starting to go in the house to turn on the TV when I heard this shot."

"Did you turn on the television?"

"Sure did. Seems to me I missed the first couple of minutes of it. Remember I was mad that I turned it on in the middle of a commercial."

Mason said, "Your testimony may be very valuable, Mr. Holbrook. There was just the one shot?"

"Just the one shot. That's why I figured it wasn't a backfire. Usually you get a backfire and there'll be an interval of a second or two and then two or three more backfires, and then an interval and maybe one big backfire—something like that. This was just the one single explosion."

Mason said, "I'm going to ask you to come to court as a witness. Do you have any objection?"

"Well, I don't want to get mixed up in things," Holbrook said. "But I don't want to be a party to an injustice."

Mason glanced at Paul Drake. "Would your wife's sister get a kick out of seeing your picture in the paper?"

Holbrook grinned. "Now, I'll say she would! She's a good sport. If she thought that there'd been a murder committed out there and she just missed it— Well, she'd get a kick out of it, but . . ." And here the smile left Holbrook's face. "I'm not so sure about Doris."

"That's your wife?" Mason asked.

"That's my wife, for better or worse. She's it."

Holbrook was thoughtful for a moment, then went on. "She's awful nice. Good housekeeper; mighty neat and considerate—can't say that I complain, but she isn't like Edith."

"Edith is the sister?" Mason asked.

"Edith is the sister."

"You drove to the airport to meet your wife's sister?"

"That's right."

"How far do you live from the airport?"

"Takes us twenty-five minutes."

"And she arrived on the ten-fifty plane?"

"That's right."

"Then you could have hardly listened to the ten o'clock news that night," Mason said.

A sudden frown creased Holbrook's forehead. "Now, wait a minute. Wait a minute," he said. "Oh yes, the plane was a little late. I remember we called up about ten o'clock. They said the plane would be fifteen minutes late. I'm pretty sure I watched both the nine o'clock and the ten o'clock news that night."

"You're sure about the nine o'clock news?"

"That's right. I was mad because I missed the first minute or two of the nine o'clock news, so I turned the set on again at ten."

Mason said to Della Street, "I think we're going to have to rely on Mr. Holbrook as a witness, Della."

Della Street nodded, handed Mason the subpoena.

Mason said, "Just to make it formal, Mr. Holbrook, I'm

giving you a subpoena. This is made out for ten o'clock tomorrow morning. If you'll just be in court at ten o'clock, I don't think we're going to detain you very long because I think the prosecution is about ready to rest its case."

"Well, whatever's right is right," Holbrook said. "I just thought you ought to know about it. I called the office and they said you were in court but the Drake Detective Agency was investigating anything in connection with the case, so I told my story down there at the agency. That was right?"

"That was right," Mason said.

"Well, I was awfully glad to meet you people. I guess I didn't get your name, young lady."

"Della Street," she said, "Mr. Mason's confidential secretary, and have been for many years."

"I figured as much," Holbrook said, putting forth a big bony paw. "Even if you look young, you seem to know what's what. Pleased to meet you, Miss Street."

Then Holbrook solemnly shook hands with Mason and with Paul Drake. Della Street held the door open and Holbrook walked out.

Mason waited until the door had clicked shut; then he executed a little jig, grabbed Della Street around the waist, whirled her into a few steps of a dance, then released her to grab Paul Drake's hand and pump it up and down.

"Saved by the bell!" he said.

"You think that'll do it?" Drake asked.

"That'll do it," Mason said. "That's going to create a reasonable doubt."

"Suppose the prosecution comes up with someone who swears the shot was later?"

Mason grinned and said, "I'll then claim there were *two* shots, and the prosecution can't prove which shot was the fatal shot from the standpoint of time."

"It'll create a reasonable doubt?" Drake asked.

"It'll do better than that," Mason said. "It'll probably result in a verdict of acquittal on the theory that Dutton is telling the truth and Palmer was dead when he got there. Dutton just walked into a trap."

"It still would have been a lot better if he hadn't taken that gun and hidden it," Drake said.

Mason's face lost its smile. "Are you telling me?" he said. "I'm going to have to do quite a bit of arguing to get around that, but I'm going to make it appear that when he saw that gun, he naturally thought the woman he loved was involved."

"Desere Ellis?"

Mason nodded.

"Going to let him say that he's in love with her on the witness stand?" Drake asked.

Mason shook his head. "Heavens, no, I'm not going to let him *say* it. I'm going to let him try to keep from saying it; and then when the district attorney takes him on cross-examination, it's all going to come out and come out reluctantly. We'll have a romantic and dramatic scene in the courtroom."

"And, I take it," Drake said, "no defense attorney ever got an unjust verdict when there was a romantic and a dramatic scene in a courtroom?"

"Not one involving heartthrobs," Mason said, "and this is going to involve heartthrobs, orange blossoms, wedding bells and what have you.

"Come on, we're closing up the shop and I'm going to buy you folks the best dinner to be had anywhere in the city—a dinner with all the frills, including ice-cold vintage champagne."

Chapter 18

The next morning as Judge Alvarado took his place on the bench and looked over the courtroom, it was quite apparent that the prosecution was discussing strategy on a matter which they considered to be of considerable importance.

Bailey and Hamilton Burger had their heads together in a whispered conference, as soon as the bailiff had rapped his gavel and Judge Alvarado had seated himself on the bench.

"The case of People versus Kerry Dutton," Judge Alvarado said. "The defendant is in court; the jurors are all present. It is so stipulated, gentlemen?"

"So stipulated," Perry Mason said.

"Yes, Your Honor," Hamilton Burger said. "It is so stipulated. May we have just a moment?"

Again there was a whispered conference; then Burger nodded his head somewhat reluctantly, apparently.

Immediately Bailey jumped to his feet. "If the Court please, that concludes the evidence of the prosecution. We rest our case."

A murmur of surprise ran through the spectators in the courtroom.

Judge Alvarado frowned. "It would have been perhaps fairer to the defense if the decision had been announced at the close of the courtroom session yesterday."

"We didn't know it at that time. We have just this minute reached our decision," Bailey said.

"Very well," Judge Alvarado said. "I will, however, be willing to grant the defense a reasonable recess so that it may meet this somewhat unexpected development."

"If the Court please," Mason said, arising and smiling at

the jury, "the defense is not only willing but eager to proceed immediately."

"Very well," Judge Alvarado said. "Go ahead."

"And we do not wish to make an opening statement at this time," Mason said. "Our first witness is Desere Ellis."

"Come forward to the stand, Miss Ellis," Judge Alvarado said. "You have already been sworn and so it is not necessary for you to take an oath once more."

Desere Ellis came forward. This time she met the defendant's eyes with a quick flicker of a smile; then seated herself on the witness stand and turned to face Perry Mason.

"You are, of course, acquainted with the defendant and have known him for some time?" Mason asked.

"Yes."

"Did the defendant ever give you a gun?"

"He loaned me a gun, yes."

Mason said, "I show you the People's Exhibit A-G, a Smith and Wesson snub-nosed, thirty-eight-caliber revolver, number K524967, and ask you whether or not you have ever seen this gun before?"

"That is the gun that he gave me."

"Did he make any statement to you when he gave you the gun?"

"Yes. There had been some rather offensive telephone calls from a person who did not disclose his name and I was a little apprehensive."

"Now, was there any conversation specifically about the ownership of this gun which took place when it was handed to you?"

"Objected to as incompetent, irrelevant, and immaterial and as a self-serving declaration," Bailey said.

"I am simply asking for a conversation which was part of the *res gestae* of this particular transaction," Mason said. "It is a part of the transaction itself and it took place far in advance of this murder."

"That doesn't keep it from being a self-serving declaration, nor does it make it competent or relevant to the case at bar," Bailey said.

"I think I'll overrule the objection," Judge Alvarado said. "It is always my policy to give the defendant as much leeway as possible in cases of this sort. Answer the question."

"Yes," Desere Ellis said, "he said that it was his gun, one he had bought some time ago but had no use for."

"Did he show you anything about using it?"

"Yes, he took the shells out of it and taught me how to point it and pull the trigger."

"You knew then that it was a double-action revolver?"

"I beg your pardon, I don't understand."

"In other words, by pulling the trigger all the way back, you cock the hammer and then after the hammer has passed a certain point, it comes down on the firing pin so the shell is exploded and at that time the cylinder advances," Mason said. "The effect of this action is such that you can pull the trigger six times and fire six shots."

"Yes."

"What I am getting at," Mason said, "is that this gun he gave you was not an automatic; it was a revolver. In other words, the cylinder rotated."

"Yes."

"And what happened to this gun?" Mason asked.

"I kept it in a drawer in my bedroom, in a nightstand."

"When did you last see it?"

"I last saw it some two or three days before the twenty-first of September."

"Two or three days before the date of the murder?"

"Yes, sir."

"And when did you next look for the gun after that?"

"It was, I believe, either the twenty-third or the twenty-fourth of September."

"And how did you happen to look for it?"

"You asked me about it and I went to get it for you and then found it was gone."

"Cross-examine," Mason said.

Hamilton Burger, who seldom had an opportunity to cross-examine Mason's witnesses, inasmuch as Mason usually made a practice of winning his cases before the prosecution rested and by bringing out his defense from the prosecution's own witnesses, seized upon the opportunity with the eager avidity of a bird pouncing upon a hapless worm.

"What make was the gun that the defendant gave you?" he asked.

"What make?"

"Yes, who manufactured it? Was it a Colt, a Smith and Wesson, a Harrington and Richardson, a—"

She shook her head. "I don't know the brand, Mr. Burger."

"You don't know the manufacturer's name?"

"No, sir."

"You don't know the serial number?"

"No, sir."

"Yet when Perry Mason held this gun up in front of you and asked if you had seen this Smith and Wesson gun, number K524967 and you said it was the gun the defendant had given you, you were swearing to facts you didn't know. Is that right?"

"I relied upon Mr. Mason. It looked exactly like the gun Mr. Dutton had given me."

"Looked like it," Hamilton Burger sneered. "How many guns have you had in your possession?"

"Just the one."

"You never looked at the number on this gun?"

"No, sir."

"You don't even know where the number is located, do you?"

"No, sir."

"You say it looked like this gun," Hamilton Burger said, holding up the weapon. "People's Exhibit A-G?"

"Yes."

"Exactly like it?"

"As nearly as I can tell, exactly like it."

"Do you know how these weapons are made?"

"What do you mean?"

"You know that they are made by machinery and then assembled?"

"I assume as much."

"And do you know that there are hundreds—thousands—perhaps hundreds of thousands of guns of this exact make and model, guns which look exactly like this?"

"Well, I . . . I suppose so."

"You didn't notice any distinguishing marks on the gun which the defendant gave you, no scratches of any sort?"

"No, sir."

"So, for all you know, the defendant could have had half a dozen guns and simply handed you any one of these guns, told you that it was his and still been carrying another gun in his pocket?"

"Well, I . . . I can't identify this specific gun."

"Exactly," Burger said, "all you know is that the defendant gave you *a* gun. You don't know that he gave you *this* gun."

"I can't swear to it."

"Then you can't testify to it," Hamilton Burger said. "You're here to swear, not to guess."

The witness was at a loss for any answer.

Hamilton Burger tried a new attack.

"Prior to the disappearance of this gun, had the defendant called on you?"

"He had been at my apartment, yes."

"And while he was there, had he made some excuse to go to the place where you kept this gun? Think carefully now."

"He had a fight with Fred Hedley."

"Where did that fight take place?"

"In my apartment."

"I mean where in your apartment?"

"It wound up in my bedroom."

"In your *bedroom*!"

"Yes."

"That's where you kept this gun?"

"Yes, sir."

"And the defendant was in there?"

"Yes, sir."

"What was the date of this fight?"

"The twenty-first of September."

"The night of the murder?"

"Yes, sir."

"So on the night of the murder the defendant made an excuse to go to the room where you kept this gun, created a diversion there, then ran out and when next you looked in the bedroom for this gun, it was gone. Is that right?"

"Well, it wasn't—"

"Yes or no, please."

"Well . . . yes."

"That's all!" Burger announced.

Mason said, "One question on redirect. Who started the fight?"

"Fred Hedley."

"Who ran into the bedroom where you kept the gun?"

"He did."

"Fred Hedley?"

"Yes."

"That's all," Mason said, smiling, "and our next witness will be the defendant, Kerry Dutton."

Mason turned to Dutton. "It's up to you," he whispered. "If you can put it across, you're out, and if you can't, you're convicted."

"I'll put it across," Dutton promised, and strode to the place in front of the witness stand where he held up his hand; was sworn; took the witness chair and turned to face Perry Mason.

Mason led the witness along skillfully, showing his name, his occupation, his acquaintance with the father of Desere Ellis, the death of the father, the provisions of the will by which Dutton became trustee of a so-called spendthrift trust.

"What was the value of the various securities which you received under this trust at the time you received them?"

"Approximately one hundred thousand dollars."

"And the term of the trust under the will was how long?"

"Until the beneficiary, Desere Ellis, became twenty-seven years of age."

"And there was a provision in the will that the trust was created because her father believed she was at an impressionable age in life; that she was overly sympathetic, particularly to lost causes, and that he felt she needed to be protected from herself?"

"Yes, sir."

"And did you discuss with Miss Ellis the manner in which you proposed to administer the trust?"

"Yes, sir."

"The first conversation," Mason said, holding up the index finger of his left hand, "let's have the first conversation. What did you tell her?"

"I told her what the income from this money would be; that it wouldn't support her in the rather expensive style to which she had been accustomed; that she would undoubtedly be married prior to the termination of the trust, and that I proposed to give the money to her in such a way that she would have approximately equal monthly installments for four years. That this would enable her to have a good wardrobe, to travel, to keep herself in a position to meet the right sort of people."

"In other words," Mason said, "to exhibit herself favorably on the matrimonial market?"

Dutton frowned. "That wasn't what I said."

"How much have you given her on an average each year during the time the trust has been in effect?"

"Approximately twenty-four thousand dollars."

"What is the value of the money in the trust fund at the present time," Mason asked, "the market value of the securities and the cash on hand?"

"Approximately two hundred and fifty thousand dollars," Dutton said.

Judge Alvarado leaned forward sharply. "What was that figure?" he asked.

"Approximately two hundred and fifty thousand dollars."

"How does that happen?" Judge Alvarado asked. "You had a trust fund of one hundred thousand dollars. You dispersed ninety-six thousand dollars?"

"Yes, Your Honor, but under the provisions of the trust, I was empowered to make investments, to buy and sell securities and to keep the trust in a healthy condition."

"And you made that much profit?"

"After taxes," Dutton said.

"Well," Judge Alvarado remarked, "you certainly showed remarkable ability."

"Did you," Mason asked, "tell the beneficiary the extent of the trust funds?"

"No."

"Why not?"

"Objected to as incompetent, irrelevant and immaterial," Hamilton Burger said.

"I think I will sustain that objection," Judge Alvarado said. "The answer is that he didn't tell the beneficiary. To your knowledge, did she have any idea of the nature and the extent of the trust fund?"

"No."

"Now then," Mason said, "the trust fund was created so that you could protect her from herself."

"Yes."

"Did you feel that if she knew the exact amount of the trust, that it would tend to defeat the purposes of the trust; that she would extravagantly espouse some lost cause and—"

"Your Honor, Your Honor," Hamilton Burger literally shouted, "this question is viciously leading and suggestive. I object to it. It is incompetent, irrelevant and immaterial."

"Sustained," Judge Alvarado snapped. "Counsel will refrain from this sort of question."

However, the jurors, exchanging astonished glances, showed that the point had registered and made a deep impression on them.

"Now then," Mason said, "did you know and do you know a Fred Hedley?"

"Yes."

"What was his relationship to Desere Ellis?"

"He was described by her on occasion as her fiancé."

"Did you approve of him?"

"I did not."

"Why?"

"Objected to as incompetent, irrelevant and immaterial," Burger said.

Judge Alvarado hesitated. "I think," he said, "I am beginning to see a pattern in counsel's questions. A pattern which may well be pertinent to the defense. I am going to overrule the objection. The answer will be limited as to the state of mind of this witness. Further, it will be limited to the actions of the witness in connection with the trust fund."

"Answer the question," Mason said.

"I felt that he was a fortune hunter."

"And was it because of him that you refrained from telling Deserc Ellis— Just a minute," Mason said, as he saw Hamilton Burger on his feet, "I'll reframe that question. Did that idea on your part have anything to do with your actions in connection with giving information of the amount of the trust fund? You can answer that yes or no."

"Objected to," Hamilton Burger said.

"Overruled," Judge Alvarado said.

"Yes, it did."

"In connection with the trust fund, did you have securities of a company known as the Steer Ridge Oil and Refining Company?"

"I did."

"Those had been part of the original securities transmitted to you as trustee under the terms of the will?"

"Yes."

"What did you do with those securities?"

"I sold them."

"Did you ever discuss that sale with the beneficiary?"

"No."

"What had she told you about the Steer Ridge stock?"

"She was very much interested in it. She became somewhat excited because they had sent her a brochure telling about the valuable oil properties they had under lease. She knew that her father had been enthusiastic about the stock."

"And did she make any request to you in connection with those securities?"

"She asked me to hang on to them."

"But you disregarded her request?"

"Yes."

"And then what?"

"Well, I sold the securities and . . . well, after a while I reinvested."

"In those same securities?"

"Yes, in a block of that same stock."

"Why?"

"I had a tip that— Well, I had reason to believe that there might be a proxy fight, and they might turn out to be a good investment if two different factions were going to fight for control of the company."

"How much did you buy?"

"Twenty thousand shares."

"In connection with those securities, did you have any contact with the decedent, Rodger Palmer?"

"I talked with him over the telephone, yes."

"And what was the nature of that conversation?"

"Palmer told me that he had been in touch with Desere Ellis; that he had been trying to get a proxy to vote her shares in the Steer Ridge Oil and Refining Company; that she had referred him to me; that if I would co-operate with him it would be possible for us to greatly enhance the value of the securities held by Miss Ellis or for her benefit."

"Just what did he want in that connection?"

"He said that it would be necessary for us to have a meeting in great secrecy."

"Did you arrange such a meeting?"

"After he told me that if I would see that he had the proxy for twenty thousand shares, and an unsecured loan of five thousand dollars, he would see that Fred Hedley would be placed in such a position that it would be impossible for him to marry Desere Ellis, I told him a meeting might be arranged."

"And what happened?"

"He told me that at a certain time on the evening of September twenty-first, I was to call a certain number; that that would be the number of a pay station; that the person who answered that number would give me another telephone number to call which would be the number of another pay station; that if I would call that number, I would be advised where to go in order to meet him."

"Did you make such a call as the first one?"

"Yes."

"And what were you told?"

"I was given the number of the other pay station, the number which I was to call."

"Was that the decedent, Rodger Palmer, with whom you were talking?"

"I don't know. The voice sounded disguised. It sounded like a man trying to talk in a high-pitched voice. It could even have been a woman. I thought at the time it was a man. Thinking back on it now I am not so sure."

"And you called the next number?"

"Yes."

"And what happened then?"

"A voice told me to go to the seventh tee at the Barclay Country Club, to be there just as soon as I could get there; that there had been some mix-up in time schedule; that the man I was to meet was going to be forced to leave in just a few minutes; that I was to get there at the earliest possible instant."

"Was anything said in any of these conversations about money?"

"Yes, I was to have five thousand dollars with me. If the information that was to be given me was as represented, I was to pay over the five thousand dollars."

"At the time of this telephone conversation, did you have occasion to notice the witness, Tom Fulton, who has previously testified?"

"Yes, sir, I saw him, but, of course, at that time, I had no idea he was taking any personal interest in me. I thought he was simply someone who was in a hurry to use the telephone. He came up to the telephone booth and made some sort of signs to me and I motioned him to go away."

"Subsequently, did you know that he was following you?"

"No, sir."

"You left the phone booth in a hurry and went through some red lights and a boulevard stop?"

"I'm afraid that I was in such a hurry that I violated several sections of the vehicle code."

"And went to the country club?"

"Yes."

"You are a member of that club?"

"Yes."

"Did you know that you had been followed to that club, or followed part of the way?"

"No, sir."

"What did you do?"

"I parked my car, used my key and went in. I looked around for the night watchman but didn't see him. I hurried out on the links."

"You were familiar with the location of the seventh tee?"

"Yes."

"What did you do?"

"I hurried out there and looked around; saw no one, but finally noticed a dark object lying on the ground. I bent over that object and it was the body of this man, Rodger Palmer."

"You knew him at the time?"

"I had not seen him previously. I had talked with him over the telephone. That was all."

"How many times?"

"Several times. First, after he had requested Desere Ellis to give her proxy and she had referred him to me. He had called me and then I had had several conversations with him over the telephone concerning a suggestion that I pay him for this information which he offered to give me."

"What time was it when you got to the Barclay Country Club?"

"It was just a few minutes before ten."

"What did you do after you discovered the body?"

"I looked around— That is, I wanted to make sure he was dead."

"And when you did make sure, then what did you do?"

"I got to my feet. My right foot encountered a hard object. I bent over to find out what it was, and saw that it was a gun."

"And then what did you do?"

"I realized it was my own gun and suddenly became panic-stricken."

"And what did you do?"

"I left the country club. I drove down the road for a short distance, threw the gun under a culvert where I hoped it would never be discovered; went to Ensenada in Mexico and registered at the Siesta del Tarde Auto Court under the name Frank Kerry."

"Frank is one of your names?"

"Yes, my full name is Frank Kerry Dutton."

"You recognized the gun as your own?"

"I thought it was mine, yes."

"And you knew you had given that gun to Desere Ellis?"

"Yes."

"Were you trying to protect Desere Ellis in—"

"Objected to," Hamilton Burger said, "incompetent, irrelevant and immaterial, argumentative, leading and suggestive."

"Sustained," Judge Alvarado said.

"Cross-examine," Mason snapped.

Hamilton Burger, the district attorney, masked his true feelings behind a façade of extreme courtesy as he arose and approached the witness.

"I have a few questions," he said. "Simply for the purpose of clarifying your story in my own mind and for the jury, Mr. Dutton, I take it you have no objections?"

"Certainly not," Dutton said.

It was quite apparent that Hamilton Burger, having been warned by Mason, would make every effort to tear him to pieces, and the defendant was agreeably surprised by this attitude on the part of the prosecutor.

"We'll start with finding the body," Hamilton Burger said. "What time was it that you arrived at the seventh tee? I believe you said it was a minute or two after ten?"

"Yes, sir."

"Well, we should be able to clarify it a little better than that," Burger said. "You were in a hurry?"

135

"Yes."

"Is there, by any chance, a clock on the dashboard of your automobile?"

"There is."

"Was it accurate on the night in question?"

"I try to keep it accurate, yes, sir."

"Well, now," Burger said, smiling, "from the manner in which you make that statement, I gather that it is a habit of yours to be punctual and to know what time it is?"

"Yes, sir."

"So you keep your clock accurate at all times?"

"I try to, yes."

"Now, having made an appointment for that night and being in a great hurry, you undoubtedly looked at your clock several times while you were driving from the telephone booth to the golf club—you must have."

"I'm quite sure I did," Dutton said, matching the district attorney's affable courtesy.

"Exactly," Hamilton Burger said, his voice low and well modulated, "so you must be able to tell the jury what you mean by a minute or two after ten?"

"I would say that it was one minute before ten when I entered the golf club. I think I arrived there and had parked the car at one minute after ten."

"I see," Hamilton Burger said, "and how long did it take you to get to the seventh tee?"

"I would say about three minutes."

"So you arrived at the seventh tee at exactly four minutes after ten?"

"We could give or take a few seconds, but for practical purposes, right around four minutes after ten."

"So it takes you about three minutes to go from the seventh tee to the clubhouse?"

"Yes."

"Now, you have heard the detective, Tom Fulton, testify that you left the golf club at ten-twenty-two?"

"Yes, sir."

"Did you, by any chance, look at the clock on your automobile when you left?"

"I was rather excited. I didn't look at the clock at that exact moment. No, I remember I did look at it when I stopped the car at the culvert."

"And what time was it then?"

Dutton smiled. "Frankly, I have forgotten, Mr. Burger. The time registered with me but it didn't seem to have any particular significance. I do remember, however, looking at the clock. I think it was right around ten-twenty-five or something like that. I am not sure."

"Why did you glance at the clock?"

"Just a mechanical reflex, I guess."

"I see," Hamilton Burger said. And then suddenly added, "Oh, by the way, had you made up your mind to go to Ensenada at that time?"

"I was thinking of it, yes."

"So," Burger said casually, "you probably were checking the time to figure about how long it would take you to make the trip."

"I could have been, yes."

"Well, that sounds very reasonable," Burger said.

Dutton nodded.

"Now, let's see," Burger went on, "you got to the seventh tee at four minutes past ten. You were expecting to meet Rodger Palmer there, and, of course, expected him to be alive?"

"Yes, sir."

"There was a glow in the sky, that is, you could see the reflection of the lights of the city?"

"Yes, sir, quite a glow."

"Enough light for you to walk by and find your way?"

"Yes, sir."

"Not bright light, but a diffused light such as one would naturally expect on a golf course from the lights of the city reflected by the atmospheric impurities?"

"Yes, sir."

"And if Rodger Palmer had been standing up to meet you when you reached the seventh tee, he would have stood silhouetted against the skyline?"

"Yes, sir."

137

"Then you must have suspected something was wrong almost immediately on reaching the seventh tee and failing to see him?"

"I think I did. I think that's what started me looking around."

"Looking around?"

"Yes."

"What do you mean by looking around?"

"Well, taking a few steps; looking on the ground."

"Looking *on the ground*?" Hamilton Burger said, his voice suddenly changing. "So, you began looking for the man you were to meet on the ground?"

"Well, I was looking around. He wasn't standing up. He had to be someplace if he was there."

"I see," Hamilton Burger said, "so within a few seconds of the time you arrived at the seventh tee you began looking for him on the ground?"

"I didn't say within a few seconds."

"No, you didn't," Hamilton Burger said, "but it follows as a necessary inference. You expected him to meet you. You looked around; you didn't see him outlined against the lights of the horizon. So you started looking around. Now, it didn't take you over two or three seconds to ascertain that he wasn't standing up silhouetted against the horizon. Isn't that right?"

"Yes, sir."

"So then, right away, you began looking around— You'll pardon me, Mr. Dutton, I want to be fair with you. I want to see that the jury understands your story, that's all. It was within a few seconds, wasn't it?"

"Yes, I guess it was."

"So, you were then looking on the ground at least by five minutes after ten?"

"I guess I must have been, yes."

"And as soon as you looked on the ground, you discovered the body?"

"Well, not right away."

"But within a matter of seconds, eight or ten seconds?"

"I don't know that it was eight or ten seconds."

"Well, let's time it," Hamilton Burger said. "Just get up from the witness stand, if you will, and start walking around in a circle. I'll consult my watch and let you know when ten seconds are up."

The witness got up from the stand and started walking. He made a circle, then another circle.

"That's ten seconds," Hamilton Burger said. "Now then, considering your starting place as being at the seventh tee, would the body have been within that circle?"

"Well, perhaps a little wider circle."

"Then, perhaps it was twenty seconds after you started looking around that you found him?"

"I would say so. Perhaps even as much as thirty seconds."

"Thirty seconds would be the extreme limit?"

"I would say so, yes, sir."

"All right, then, within that circle that you made in thirty seconds, your foot struck against something?"

"Well, I saw something dark and prodded it with my foot."

"And found it was a body?"

"Yes, sir."

"And immediately dropped to your knees?"

"Yes, sir."

"Now then," Hamilton Burger said, "that was within thirty seconds. Let's say that you dropped to your knees— Oh, let's give you plenty of time, Mr. Dutton. Let's say that by six minutes past ten you had dropped to your knees by the side of the body."

"Yes, sir."

"That seems fair to you?"

"I think it is very fair."

"And you ascertained at once the man was dead?"

"Well, within a few seconds."

"Ten seconds again, Mr. Dutton?"

"I would say so, yes. Well within ten seconds."

"Now then," Hamilton Burger said, "you ascertained the man was dead and then what?"

"Well, I was just going to run and call the police when

my foot struck against something heavy and I reached down and saw it was this gun."

"And then what did you do?"

"I recognized the gun as mine."

"You were sure it was yours?"

"I felt certain it was."

"So then what?"

"Then I suddenly realized I was in a peculiar position."

"One would certainly say so," Hamilton Burger said. "In fact, that's the understatement of the week. You *were* in a *most peculiar* position."

"Yes, sir."

"So you wanted to stop and take a while to think it over?"

"Yes, sir."

"Now, eventually you reached a decision and decided to leave the golf club without reporting the fact that you had found the body to the police?"

"Yes, sir."

"Once you reached that decision, you hurried from the seventh tee, out through the clubhouse, crossed to where your car was parked, jumped in and drove away?"

"Yes, sir."

"Now then, we have that time fixed," Hamilton Burger said. "That was ten-twenty-two. Now, by ten-o-six you had found the body and found the gun; that left you with an interval of over *fifteen minutes*, Mr. Dutton."

"Well, I didn't think it was that long."

"The indisputable evidence shows that it *was* that long, Mr. Dutton. An interval of fifteen minutes, during which time you were sitting by the corpse, holding that gun."

"It *couldn't* have been that long."

"What else were you doing?" Burger asked.

"I— Nothing else."

"Fifteen minutes," Hamilton Burger said. "A quarter of an hour. What were you trying to do, Mr. Dutton?"

"I was trying to clarify the situation."

"Were you, perhaps, concealing any evidence?"

"Certainly not. I wouldn't do that."

"But you knew the gun was evidence?"

"I assumed it was."

"And you concealed that."

"I took it with me."

"And concealed it in a culvert?"

"Yes, sir."

"So then you *did* conceal evidence?"

"Well, yes."

"Then there's no need in assuming a self-righteous attitude in front of this jury," Hamilton Burger said, "that you wouldn't conceal evidence. So, I'm going to ask you again, what you were doing during those fifteen long minutes, during that quarter of an hour that you sat there in the dark by the corpse?"

"I don't know. I was trying to adjust myself."

"Now, you could see the sky. That was rather well lighted?"

"Yes, the horizon was lighted."

"But the ground was dark?"

"Well, not too dark."

"But dark enough so that you didn't see the body immediately?"

"I saw something dark."

"But you have just told us that it took from twenty to thirty seconds; in your own words, you were walking around for perhaps thirty seconds."

"Well, it wasn't that long. It was— I'll go back to my original statement that it was eight or ten seconds."

"Then you want to change your testimony that it was not thirty seconds?"

"I think the thirty seconds was an estimate of time that you placed on it. I said it was longer than ten seconds; that it might have been twenty seconds and you said you would give me thirty seconds to be sure and be fair."

"Yes, yes," Hamilton Burger said, "then your own estimate was twenty seconds?"

"Yes, sir."

"But *now* you say you think it was less than ten seconds."

"Well, after all, I didn't carry a stopwatch."

"That's right," Hamilton Burger said, "you didn't carry a stopwatch but you did testify to this jury under oath that you thought it was longer than ten seconds; that it might have been twenty seconds."

"Well, yes."

"Now you insist that it was under ten seconds."

"I think it could have been."

"Which was right?" Hamilton Burger asked, his voice taking on an edge, "ten seconds or twenty seconds?"

"I would say nearer ten seconds."

"Now, you picked up this gun?"

"Yes."

"And thought it was yours?"

"Yes."

"What made you think so?"

"Well, I saw it was a Smith and Wesson revolver of exactly the same type I had purchased."

"You *saw* it was a Smith and Wesson revolver?"

"Yes, sir."

"How could you do that if it was so dark you couldn't see the corpse for a matter of ten or twenty seconds? How in the world could you tell the make of the gun?"

"I had a small pocket flashlight."

"You *what*?" Hamilton Burger exclaimed, as though the defendant had just admitted to murder.

"I had a small pocket flashlight."

"Well, why in the world didn't you tell us about that?"

"Nobody asked me."

"Oh, you had a pocket flashlight with you and you didn't tell us about it because no one asked you."

"That's right."

"Do you have any other incriminating admissions to make that you have hitherto withheld because nobody has asked you?"

"I don't consider that an incriminating admission."

"You don't!" Hamilton Burger said. "You now admit you had a flashlight, why didn't you use that flashlight when you were looking around?"

"Well, it was in my pocket."

"And you were too lazy to take it out of your pocket?"

"Not too lazy. I saw no need for it."

"But you started searching the ground?"

"Yes."

"For an interval of at least ten seconds?"

"Perhaps that."

"And it never occurred to you to get out the flashlight?"

"Not then."

"Did you subsequently illuminate the body with your flashlight?"

"No."

"Why not?"

"I was only trying to ascertain whether he was dead."

"Well, well, well," Hamilton Burger said, "you had a flashlight and you weren't sufficiently interested to look at the man's features to see if you knew him?"

"I had never met Rodger Palmer. I had talked with him over the telephone."

"So you assumed the body was that of Rodger Palmer?"

"Yes."

"That was only an assumption on your part?"

"Yes."

"It could have been anyone else?"

"Well, it could have been."

"You weren't curious enough to look with a flashlight?"

"No."

"In other words, you *knew* the identity of the body, didn't you, Mr. Dutton?"

"No, sir. I tell you I didn't. I only assumed it."

"But as soon as you found the gun, you looked at *it* with a flashlight?"

"Yes."

"To make sure it was a Smith and Wesson revolver?"

"Yes."

"Did you check the numbers on the gun?"

"I believe I did."

"And noticed that one shell had been fired?"

"Yes."

"And you then realized that you had left fingerprints all over the gun?"

"Yes."

"What did you do about those?"

"I took my handkerchief and wiped the gun thoroughly."

"Oh!" Hamilton Burger said. "You took your handkerchief and wiped the gun thoroughly?"

"Yes, sir."

"Thereby wiping off, not only your own fingerprints, but those of anyone else?"

"Yes, sir, I suppose so."

"And yet you have just assured us that *you* wouldn't do anything to conceal evidence, oh, no, not *you*! Why in the world did you wipe the fingerprints of the murderer off that gun?"

"I wanted to remove my own fingerprints."

"Why?"

"I was afraid—I was afraid that it was my gun and I might be connected with the murder."

"So, you had a guilty feeling that you might have been connected with the murder at least as early as six or seven minutes after ten o'clock that night?"

"Well, how would you feel if your gun had been there?"

"How would I feel?" Hamilton Burger said, drawing himself up to his full height. "I would feel that I was a law-abiding citizen and wanted the protection of the police immediately. I would have taken every possible step to have preserved the fingerprints of the murderer on that gun. I would have dashed to the nearest telephone. I would have called the police. I would have said, 'I think this is my gun. I think my fingerprints are on it, but the fingerprints of the murderer should also be on it.' I certainly wouldn't have taken a handkerchief and scrubbed the murderer's fingerprints off the gun, nor would I have stopped at a culvert and thrown the gun under a culvert, nor would I have— But, come, come, I digress, Mr. Dutton, you asked me a question and I answered it. I shouldn't have. I should be the one asking you questions. Now, after you had rubbed the fingerprints off that gun, what did you do?"

"I hurried off the golf course and got in my car."

"No, you didn't," Hamilton Burger said. "Your testimony shows that you waited another fourteen minutes. What were you doing during that fourteen minutes?"

"Well, I was rubbing the gun for one thing."

"Polishing it like mad, I suppose?"

"I polished it vigorously."

"You breathed your breath on it so that the moisture in your breath would condense on the metal and help eliminate the prints?"

"I believe I did blow on it, yes."

"Well, well," Hamilton Burger said, "and all this from a man who wouldn't presume to conceal evidence!"

Hamilton Burger shook his head as though bewildered at such depravity on the part of any human being, turned and started back to his chair. Then, as though actuated by some afterthought, turned back to the witness. "Well, let's ask you a few questions about the trust, Mr. Dutton. You say there was some hundred thousand dollars in the trust when you received it, and, after paying out a hundred thousand, there is approximately two hundred and fifty thousand left?"

"Yes, sir."

"And the Steer Ridge Oil Company stock, you sold that?"

"Yes."

"But the reason you were meeting with this man, Rodger Palmer, was to discuss making a deal with him in connection with Steer Ridge Oil Company proxies?"

"Yes, sir."

"I don't understand," Hamilton Burger said. "You had sold the Steer Ridge Oil Company stock?"

"Well, I had some other stock."

"Other stock, Mr. Dutton?"

"Yes."

"Other Steer Ridge Oil Company stock?"

"Yes."

"Well, well, tell us about that, by all means," Burger said.

"I had some stock that I had purchased myself."

"When did you purchase that?"

"The first batch was several weeks earlier, then I increased my holdings to the original amount only a few days before the strike."

"And had been holding this stock?"

"Yes."

"You sold the stock which the trust fund held in the Steer Ridge Oil Company?"

"Yes, sir. I sold that stock."

"Why?"

"Well, I thought it was highly speculative. I didn't think it was a good investment for the trust."

"But it wasn't too highly speculative to be an investment for you, yourself, as an individual?"

"I could afford to take a chance."

"I see," Burger said. "Now, with reference to the sale of the stock from the trust fund, did you sell yourself the stock from the trust fund?"

"I got my stock later and I paid the market price for it."

"But it has gone up in value?"

"Yes."

"How much has it gone up in value?"

"Quite a bit."

"What price did you credit the trust fund from the sale of that Steer Ridge stock?"

"Around ten thousand dollars."

"And what is that stock worth now?"

"Two hundred thousand."

"So you made a hundred and ninety thousand dollars' profit out of betraying the interests of the beneficiary?"

"I did nothing of the kind."

"You sold the stock from the trust fund and bought shares of that same stock yourself?"

"Yes—when I felt a proxy fight was on."

"And that stock is now worth many times what you paid for it?"

"Yes."

"And how did you justify that action as trustee, Mr. Dutton?"

146

"I felt the stock was highly speculative. I didn't buy it because I wanted it, but to protect the trust fund."

"And just how would you protect the trust fund by buying the stock in your own name?"

"I felt that I could give it back in the event the stock went up."

"Oh, I see," Hamilton Burger said, "you were buying the stock. If the stock went down you intended to absorb the loss. If the stock went up you intended to turn over the profit to the trust?"

"Well, something like that."

"Something like that!" Hamilton Burger repeated sarcastically. "Now, have you turned this stock back to the trust?"

"Yes."

"And it is because of turning this stock back to the trust that the trust now is worth two hundred and fifty thousand dollars?"

"That accounts for still further profits."

"Well, this certainly seems like financial jugglery to me," Hamilton Burger said. "Perhaps you can explain it a little better, because, after all, I'm not a financier. I believe you are a professional financial counselor, Mr. Dutton?"

"Yes, sir. I represent several clients."

"And with these other clients, do you surreptitiously sell the profitable stock to yourself?"

"These other clients are on a different basis."

"I see. They're on a basis where they ask, from time to time, for an accounting. By the way, how many accountings have you ever made to Miss Ellis?"

"I have made none."

"When did you tell her about selling the stock of the Steer Ridge Oil Company?"

"I didn't tell her."

"You didn't tell her?"

"No."

"I believe you said she asked you to hang on to that stock?"

"She wanted me to, yes."

"You didn't tell her that you had sold it?"

"No, sir."

"You didn't tell her that you had sold it to yourself?"

"No, sir."

"Nor that you were making a handsome profit on it?"

"No, sir, and the stock I purchased was not the trust stock."

"Now, you say you conveyed that stock back to the trust fund?"

"Yes."

"If this wasn't trust fund stock, why did you convey it back to the trust fund? Was it conscience money?"

"No, sir."

"Then, if it wasn't trust fund stock, why give it back? And if it *was* trust fund stock, why juggle it out of the trust and into your name?"

"I can't answer that question any better than I have."

"When did you transfer this stock to the trust fund with reference to the date of September twenty-first, about what time?"

"It was right around that time."

"Right around that time?" Hamilton Burger repeated. "How interesting! In other words, it was right around the time that this man, Rodger Palmer, started telephoning you that you transferred the stock back to the trust fund?"

"His telephone calls had nothing to do with my actions."

"Well, what else had happened at about that time?" Burger asked. "Had you, by any chance, consulted an attorney at about that time?"

The witness hesitated.

"Had you?" Hamilton Burger snapped. "Yes or no. Had you consulted an attorney at about that time?"

"Yes."

"And did you tell the attorney that you had embezzled the stock held by the trust fund?"

"I told him that I had sold certain stocks from the trust fund, stocks that I felt were going down in value."

"So you bought those same stocks?"

"The Steer Ridge shares, yes, sir."

"Are you accustomed to buying stocks that you think are going down in value?"

"I sometimes take a chance."

"You buy the stocks you think are going down in value?"

"I mean I sometimes buy speculative stocks."

"But when you buy a speculative stock, you think it is going *up* in value?"

"I hope so."

"So, when you bought this Steer Ridge stock you thought it was going *up* in value?"

"Well, I knew there was a possibility."

"Yet, as trustee, knowing that the stock was one which the beneficiary wanted you to hold; knowing that it stood a good chance of going up in value, you sold it from the trust?"

"I thought that was the best thing to do."

"The best thing for whom? For the beneficiary, or yourself?"

"For the beneficiary."

"So, later on you bought an equal amount yourself," Hamilton Burger said, musingly, "and you turned it back into the trust fund just a short time before the murder, on the advice of an attorney, and you never told the beneficiary anything about what you had done and you never made an accounting in the trust. Well, well, I'm glad I cross-examined you, Mr. Dutton, because otherwise these matters wouldn't have come out and I think the jury is interested in them. You didn't intend to tell the jurors about all this, did you?"

"I wasn't asked."

"You mean, on your direct examination, your attorney carefully avoided asking you these questions?"

"Objected to as argumentative," Perry Mason said.

"Sustained," Judge Alvarado promptly ruled.

Hamilton Burger grinned broadly at the jurors. "That concludes my cross-examination," he said, and walked back to the counsel table with the triumphant air of a man who has at last gratified a lifelong ambition.

Chapter 19

"Call Mr. Holbrook," Mason said.

George Holbrook—tall, gangling, his weather-beaten face and somewhat shambling gait claiming the attention of the jurors—took the oath and assumed his position on the witness stand.

"Do you have occasion to remember the evening of September twenty-first of this year?" Mason asked.

"I sure do."

"There was something that happened on that evening which made an impression upon you?"

"Yes, sir."

"What was it?"

"My wife's sister came to visit."

"What time did she arrive?"

"Eleven-ten was when she actually got there at the airport."

"Did you go to the airport to meet her?"

"We sure did."

"Now, calling your attention to that evening, did anything happen earlier in the evening which aroused your attention, anything at all that was out of the ordinary?"

"Yes, sir."

"What was it?"

"About nine o'clock, just right around a minute or two after nine, I heard the sound of a shot."

Hamilton Burger jumped to his feet. "I move to strike out the latter part of that answer as calling for a conclusion of the witness."

"Oh, I think the expression is common enough so we'll let it go," Judge Alvarado said. "You may cross-examine him on that point."

"Could you determine the direction of that sound?" Mason asked.

"It came from the golf links."

"Now, where is your home with reference to the golf links of the Barclay Country Club?"

"We're along a street that parallels the golf club."

"Are you familiar with the location of tee number seven?"

"Yes, sir."

"In order that there may be no mistake about it," Mason said, "I show you this map which has been introduced in evidence and ask you to notice the cross street nearest your house and the location of tee number seven."

"Yes, sir, I see it."

"About how far are you located from tee number seven?"

"About a hundred and fifty yards."

"Cross-examine," Mason said.

Hamilton Burger, on his feet, managed to get an expression of puzzled perplexity on his face as he turned to the judge and said, "If the Court please, I move to strike out this entire evidence as being incompetent, irrelevant and immaterial."

Judge Alvarado turned to Mason. "Do you care to explain your reason for calling this witness, Mr. Mason?"

"I will be glad to," Mason said. "The autopsy surgeon has testified that death occurred between nine-thirty in the evening and two-thirty A.M. the following morning.

"On cross-examination, the autopsy surgeon admitted that a doctor couldn't fix the time of death as accurately as if one was standing by with a stopwatch. Death could conceivably have occurred at nine o'clock in the evening.

"The defendant has testified that Palmer was dead when the defendant arrived on the scene. Death could well have occurred an hour earlier."

Hamilton Burger laughed and then apparently tried to control himself with an effort. "All of this," he said, "is predicated upon the fact that somebody heard an automobile backfire or a distant sonic boom or a tire blowing out; and under the persuasive influence of counsel's suggestion has been led to believe that it was a shot. And now he wants this jury to believe not only that it was *a* shot, but that it was *the* fatal shot. I submit, Your Honor, that this evidence is far too nebulous and fantastic, far too conjectural to even be cluttering up the record, let alone influencing the jury."

Judge Alvarado shook his head. "I think your argument goes to the weight rather than the admissibility of the evidence, Mr. Prosecutor. The Court is going to allow the evidence to remain in. You may, of course, further amplify your point by cross-examination."

Hamilton Burger heaved a sigh, as much as to indicate to the jury the tribulations with which a district attorney had to contend, then turned to the witness. "How do you know it was nine o'clock?" he asked.

"I was out on the porch smoking and suddenly realized it was time for a favorite television program."

"What kind of a program?"

"A newscaster and analyst."

"You say it's a favorite of yours?"

"Yes."

"Do you listen every night?"

"Almost every night, yes."

"And is that the only program that you listen to?"

"Oh, no."

"You listen to others?"

"Certainly."

"What is the nature of these other programs you listen to?"

"Well, I have two or three favorite newscasters."

"Such as what?"

"Well, I have Carleton Kenny. I try to listen to him every night."

"Oh, yes," Hamilton Burger said, "he comes on at eleven o'clock?"

"Yes, sir."

"And what others?"

"Well, two or three others."

"What was the program you were listening to at nine o'clock when you heard this sound which you took to be a shot?"

152

"I was listening to Ralph Woodley."

"Woodley?" Hamilton Burger said.

"No, no," the witness corrected himself, "I meant George Tillman."

"Now, just a minute," Hamilton Burger said. "You said first it was Woodley you were listening to."

"Well, I thought it was. That is, I suddenly realized—"

Hamilton Burger said, "You suddenly realized that one program comes on at nine o'clock and the other program comes on at ten. You said that you were listening to Woodley. *He* comes on at ten, does he not?"

"Yes, sir."

"And when I asked you to give the program you were listening to, the name Woodley slipped out before you thought."

"It was an inadvertent slip of the tongue."

"But when I asked you, you said before you had any opportunity to think that you were listening to Woodley's program."

"Yes."

"Then the shot could have been at ten o'clock."

"No, sir, the shot I heard was at nine o'clock. It was just before I went in to tune in the nine o'clock program, the last thirteen minutes of it."

Hamilton Burger, his manner suddenly magnanimous, said, "Now, Mr. Holbrook, I don't want to take any unfair advantage of you. I want you to listen carefully. Suppose I should assure you, as I do now assure you, that two reputable citizens who lived even closer to the seventh tee than you do are prepared to swear that shortly after ten o'clock, just as the Woodley program was going on the air, they heard a single pistol shot, or a sound which they interpreted as being a pistol shot coming from the direction of tee number seven. Would that testimony change your recollection and would you then state that the sound you heard, which you took to be a shot, was at ten o'clock rather than nine o'clock?"

George Holbrook seemed for a moment completely baffled. Then he slowly shook his head. "I thought it was nine o'clock," he said.

"I know you did," Hamilton Burger said, his manner suddenly sympathetic, "but you *could* have been mistaken. There was a lot of excitement that night. You went to pick up your wife's sister?"

"Yes, sir."

"And how did it happen that you didn't report the matter to the police the next morning when you read of the murder?"

"I didn't read of the murder," Holbrook said. "We decided to take a trip and we threw some things together late that night, got three or four hours' sleep and took off at daylight the next morning."

"Oh, yes," Hamilton Burger said. "And how long were you gone, Mr. Holbrook?"

"Three weeks."

"And you didn't know anything about the murder all the time you were gone?"

"I knew about it but didn't know that it had taken place on the golf links right across from our front porch, so to speak."

"So you didn't realize the importance of this sound you had heard until some three weeks later?"

"Yes, sir—sometime later."

"And then you tried to reconstruct in your mind the exact date that you had heard this shot?"

"Yes, sir."

"And the time you had heard the shot?"

"Yes, sir."

"After an interval of three weeks?"

"Yes, sir."

"Three full weeks?"

"Yes, sir."

"And it could have been while you were listening to the Woodley program, just as you said when I first asked you?"

"Yes, I thought it was the— No, no, wait a minute. The Woodley program comes on at *ten* o'clock. This was at *nine* o'clock."

Hamilton Burger smiled indulgently. "If the other witnesses fix it as being when the Woodley program was on the air, would you change your testimony once more, Mr. Holbrook, and again say that it was at the time of the Woodley program?"

"Well, I . . . I thought it was at nine o'clock."

"You thought it was," Hamilton Burger said, his manner suddenly stern, and then leaning forward and fixing the witness with a direct gaze. "You can't swear to it, can you?"

George Holbrook thought for a long moment, then said, "No, I can't positively swear to it."

"Thank you," Hamilton Burger said. "That's all."

Hamilton Burger turned away from the witness, glanced at the jury and for a moment a swift grin came over his features. Then he masked his face as though desperately trying to keep his emotions concealed from the jury.

"Very well," he said, "that's all."

Judge Alvarado said, "I have a matter which has been on the calendar for some time set for this hour and it's a matter I have to take care of. I am going to continue this case until tomorrow morning at ten o'clock. During the recess of the Court, the jurors will remember the usual admonition of the Court not to form or express any opinion as to the guilt or innocence of the defendant, and to refrain from discussing the case among yourselves, and particularly not to let anyone discuss it with you. Court is recessed until ten o'clock tomorrow."

As the spectators started filing out, Dutton leaned toward Mason. "How did I do," he asked, "—on the stand?"

Mason, putting papers in his brief case, said, "About the way I expected."

"You don't sound too enthusiastic."

Mason shook his head and said, "Go ahead and get a night's sleep and try to forget about the case. No one ever knows what a jury is going to do."

The lawyer nodded to the bailiff and to the officer who was coming forward to take Dutton into custody, managed a reassuring smile for Della Street, then walked out of the courtroom, his shoulders squared, his manner confident, his chin up, his stomach cold.

Chapter 20

Back in his office, all of Mason's assurance vanished.

"Well?" Della Street asked.

"Get Paul Drake," Mason said. "We've got to do *something* or our man is going to be convicted of first-degree murder."

"What can you do?" Della Street asked.

"We've got to do something," Mason said. "We're going to have to think up something."

"You think it's that bad?"

"I know it's that bad. The idea of Dutton bucket-shopping the stocks in the trust fund and deliberately deceiving the beneficiary into believing the trust fund was being exhausted just didn't sit well with that jury."

Della said, "Paul Drake's on his way down here now."

A few moments later, Drake's code knock sounded on the door, and Della opened it to admit the detective.

Drake raised inquiring eyebrows and Della shook her head.

Mason, pacing the floor, was engrossed in thought.

Drake slipped across to the client's chair and seated himself.

Mason said, "We've got to pull a rabbit out of the hat, Paul."

Drake nodded.

Mason continued his pacing the floor. "Something dramatic. Something that will drive home our contention."

"How does it look?" Drake asked.

"You know how it looks," Mason said, without changing the tempo of his stride or even glancing at the detective. "Hamilton Burger has alienated any sympathy the jurors might have had for the defendant. He's mixed up the only witness we had who could give any evidence that would enable us to talk about reasonable doubt."

"You've licked him so many times in front of a jury," Paul Drake said, "that I think you're being unduly pessimistic this time."

Mason shook his head. "Usually Hamilton Burger doesn't have a chance to strut his stuff. I get the witness on cross-examination and uncover some point which enables me to prove that the prosecution's theory of the case is erroneous. Before he's ready to rest his case, he doesn't have any case left.

"This time I've had to go ahead and put witnesses on the stand. Burger has had a chance to cross-examine them. The roles have been reversed. He's ripped my witnesses to pieces."

"Do you think it's true that he has two witnesses who will swear it was at ten o'clock the shot was heard?"

"It has to be true," Mason said. "Of course, I'm going to have a chance to cross-examine those witnesses and, believe me, Paul, there's something queer about that."

"What do you mean?"

"If they had been as positive as he makes them sound, he'd have put them on the witness stand as part of his case in chief. The fact that he's holding them for rebuttal indicates that he didn't intend to use them unless he had to."

"Do you think he'll just back away from the question now that he's got our witness confused?" Drake asked.

"I won't let him," Mason said. "I'm going to insist that he put those two witnesses on the stand and then I'm going to cross-examine them. I may get a break out of it, but I may not. I don't know. All I know is that the way the case looks at present, we've got a defendant who is headed for the gas chamber or for life imprisonment."

"Any suggestions?" Drake asked.

"I'm thinking of one right now."

"Such as what?"

Mason said, "Paul, start pulling wires. I want to get the latest and best metal detector that money can buy. I understand there are some new ones that are very sensitive."

"You mean mine detectors?" Drake asked.

"So-called," Mason said.

"And what do we do?"

"We go out to the Barclay Country Club and we start sweeping around the grass out in the vicinity of the seventh tee."

"Looking for what?"

"An expended cartridge."

Drake said, "Don't be silly, Perry! The murder was committed with a revolver. A revolver doesn't eject a fired cartridge."

"But a person who fires a revolver could eject a cartridge," Mason said.

"What do you mean?"

"If the murder was committed at nine o'clock, then someone who wanted a Patsy could have arranged to have Dutton out there at ten o'clock and then fired a shot the minute Dutton's car hove into sight at the golf club. Then he could have tossed the gun to the ground beside the corpse and sneaked back down through the low places where he wouldn't show against the silhouetted horizon and made his escape, leaving Dutton to hold the sack."

"And so?" Drake asked.

"And so," Mason said, "we go out on the golf course and start exploring with a mine detector."

"This is right during the busy time of the afternoon as far as that golf course is concerned," Drake said. "Court adjourned early and if we go out there now, we'll interfere with a lot of doctors and dentists, bankers and professional men playing their mid-week round of golf."

Mason nodded.

"They'd kick us out," Drake said.

"Well?" Mason asked.

Drake looked at him and grinned. "You mean you'd like to attract attention?"

"Why not?"

"It wouldn't prove anything," Drake said.

"But the fact that we were out there looking for an extra

shell would show that *we* attached considerable importance to Holbrook's testimony."

Drake thought the matter over for a while, then grinned. "I suppose you wouldn't object if the newspaper reporters knew about it?"

"Not at all," Mason said. "In fact, anything that we do might become quite newsworthy."

"The judge has instructed the jury not to read the newspapers," Drake said.

Mason looked at him and grinned, then turned to Della Street. "This, Della," he said, "is business. Go to the most exclusive, most expensive place in the city where you can get a sport outfit which will attract the roving masculine eye. Get a golfing outfit. Money is no object, but it has to be a city editor's dream—one that will look so good in a photograph, and on you, it would make a page one placement."

Della Street jumped to her feet. "Watch me go through that door," she said.

Chapter 21

A rather dignified group of afternoon golfers watched Perry Mason, Paul Drake, Della Street, and one of Drake's operatives as they marched across the golf links toward the seventh tee carrying a portable metal detector.

Mason smiled affably at the group waiting at the tee. "Don't let me disturb your game, gentlemen. We'll wait until you drive."

"Until we drive?" one of the men asked.

Mason smiled and nodded toward Drake's operative who was carrying the metal detector.

"What's that?" the golfer asked.

"You knew, of course, about the murder that had been committed here," Mason said. "We're looking for evidence."

"What sort of evidence?"

"We think perhaps there's— Well, perhaps it isn't wise to disclose my hand in advance. There's perhaps something here that will have a bearing on the case."

The golfers crowded around, their game forgotten.

"You're Perry Mason," one of the men said, "the famous attorney."

Mason bowed and smiled. "Paul Drake, my private detective, one of his operatives, and—most important of all— Miss Street, my confidential secretary."

Della Street, attired in a form-fitting short skirt which the wind whipped about her knees, gave the men her most engaging smile.

Other golfers came up.

"Well," Mason said to the operative, "we may as well go to work."

The man plugged earphones in his ears, set the electrical

dials so they were in proper balance, then started moving slowly along through the taller grass to the sides of the teeing-off place.

Within a matter of moments, fifty spectators had formed in a ring.

On the tee someone said, "It's your honors."

"To hell with the golf," the man said. "This is a lot more exciting. I'll concede every hole from here on in and pay off at that price. Let's see what's happening."

Word passed like wildfire around the links. Soon the manager of the club came hurrying out to find out what was going on.

At first he was frowningly uncompromising. Then as he saw the interest of the golfers, he became mollified and, after a few moments, hurried toward the clubhouse.

Drake said in an undertone to Perry Mason, "He's suddenly become publicity conscious, Perry. He's headed for a telephone to call the press."

"Well," Mason said in an equally low tone, "I'm certain nothing that *we* said could have prompted that idea."

"Moreover," Drake added, "he's about thirty minutes too late."

Mason gave the detective a searching look. "Your ethics are showing, Paul."

"It's all right," Drake said. "*If* my man should find anything, we'd have to tell the police about it, but there's nothing in the code of ethics which says I can't tell the press where I'm searching."

"As a lawyer," Mason said, "I couldn't use publicity in any way. It would be unethical."

Drake grinned. "I knew why you wanted *me* along on this one—at least, I thought I did."

The man with the metal detector moved slowly along, weaving the flat pan back and forth just over the surface of the grass back toward the green on the sixth hole, then down along the edge of a sand trap into the rough; back to the sand trap again, then down into the rough.

Suddenly he said, "Hey, I've got something!"

"Well, let's see what it is," Mason said.

The man held the pan of the device directly over the spot.

Drake, down on his hands and knees, felt with exploring fingertips in the grass. "I've got it," he said, and came up with an empty brass cartridge case.

Mason said jubilantly, "Drive a peg of some sort in the ground at the exact place where that was found, Paul. Let's mark it."

Drake took a small metal surveyor's stake from the place where he had been carrying it in his belt and pushed it into the ground, then tied a bright red ribbon in the loop.

"Camera?" Mason asked.

Della Street handed Mason a camera.

The lawyer circled the place, taking a dozen pictures from all different angles, showing the location with reference to all the fixed landmarks.

Then the lawyer carefully dropped the cartridge case into a pocket formed in a pocket handkerchief. Drake scratched the case. Mason examined it with a pocket magnifier.

The crowd of golfers, pushing closer, were almost breathing down the necks of the triumphant searchers.

"Just what does this mean?" one of the golfers asked.

Mason said, "It means that we now have corroboration— Well, I hadn't better discuss it here."

The lawyer looked up with a smile that was all but cherubic in its innocence. "I wouldn't want to be accused of trying to influence public thinking," he said. "You can look in the papers tomorrow and find much more than I am in a position to tell you now."

Drake touched Mason's arm. "Let's go where we can talk," he said.

Mason nodded, took Paul Drake's arm and smiled affably at the circle of golfers.

"If you'll pardon us just for a minute," he said, "we have a matter to discuss."

Mason led Drake through the circle which opened for them and over toward the rough.

"Well?" Mason asked.

Drake said, "Look, Perry, it's not up to me to tell you

how to try a lawsuit, but you're going to get a terrific amount of publicity out of this."

"Well?" Mason asked.

"And it's going to backfire," Drake said. "If we had found a cartridge that had been taken from a revolver and thrown away, we'd have had something; but this is a shell that has been ejected from an automatic—a thirty-two caliber automatic at that—and the murder gun is a thirty-eight-caliber snub-nosed Smith and Wesson revolver."

"And so?" Mason asked.

"So," Drake said, "no matter how you look at it, the thing can't be evidence."

"What do you mean it can't be evidence?" Mason said. "It was here. It's an expended cartridge."

"But there weren't *two* guns."

"How do you know there weren't?" Mason asked.

"Well, of course, we don't know, but we can surmise."

"Leave the surmising for the district attorney," Mason said. "You and I have just discovered a most important piece of evidence."

"Well, of course, it could be made to fit into your theory," Drake said, "but it would take a lot of high-pressure salesmanship to convince the jury that it meant anything."

"After all," Mason told him, "a lawyer is, or should be, an expert in the field of high-pressure salesmanship. Come on, let's get back to complete the search."

"What do you mean, complete the search?"

"Well," Mason said, "we wouldn't want to call it off when the search was incomplete."

"How much do you intend to search?"

"Well, quite a bit," Mason said. "We want to be sure there's nothing else here."

"I get you," Drake said, wearily. "You're going to stall along until the newspapers start covering what we're doing."

Mason's eyes became wide. "Why, Paul Drake, how you talk," he said. "We're doing nothing of the sort. We're simply completing the search."

Drake said suddenly, "Look here, Perry, did *you* drop that cartridge case so my man could find it?"

"Of course not."

"Did Della?"

"You'll have to ask her."

"The district attorney will claim you planted it either in advance or while we were searching."

"Can he prove it?" Mason asked.

"Good Lord, I hope not!"

"So do I," Mason said. "Come on, Paul, let's get back to work."

The circle of interested spectators opened for the lawyer and the detective. Mason said to the operative, "All right, I think we've found what we were looking for, but let's just make sure there's nothing else here. Let's complete the search."

Slowly, a step at a time, they moved around the golf course until Drake nudged Mason's arm.

The lawyer looked up to see a newspaper reporter and a photographer with a camera and flashgun hurrying toward them.

"Keep right on with your search," Mason told the operative with the metal detector, "although I think we've just about covered the ground here. I think we have everything we need."

The reporter hurried up, pushed his way through the circle of spectators, said to Mason, "What's going on here, Mr. Mason?"

Mason frowned as though the interruption were unwelcome. "We're looking for evidence," he said shortly.

"What sort of evidence?"

Mason thought for a long moment, then grudgingly admitted, "Well, as you can see for yourself, it's metallic evidence."

Someone in the crowd said, "They've already found one empty cartridge case."

"An empty cartridge case?" the reporter asked.

Mason nodded.

"May we see it?"

164

Mason said, "We're trying to preserve it as intact as possible."

He took a handkerchief from his pocket, carefully unfolded it and showed the reporter the cartridge case nesting in the cloth. "Don't touch it," he warned. "I doubt if anyone can find any fingerprints on it, but we certainly don't want the evidence contaminated."

The reporter pulled out some folded newsprint from his pocket, took a soft, 6-B pencil and started scribbling.

The photographer fed flashbulbs into the gun on his camera. He shot two closeup pictures of the cartridge, then backed away and took two pictures of the group, carefully including Della Street.

Mason very gently folded the handkerchief back over the cartridge case and put it in his pocket.

"Well," he said, "I think we have completed the search. I guess we found everything that was here."

He waited an appreciable moment, then added, "I may say that we've found everything that we thought was here."

"Just what caused you to think that cartridge was here, Mr. Mason?" the reporter asked.

Mason gave the question careful consideration. "There were," he said at length, "two shots. One at nine o'clock, one at approximately one hour later. Two shots mean two cartridges. There was only one empty cartridge in the gun which the police contend was the murder weapon."

"But that was a revolver," the reporter said. "This cartridge case that you have was ejected from an automatic."

"Exactly," Mason said, with an enigmatic smile, and then added, "I don't think I should be giving an interview at this time. Come on, folks, let's go."

Chapter 22

Judge Alvarado surveyed the crowded courtroom with something of a frown. "The jurors seem to be all present, and the defendant is in court," he said. "I trust that the jurors have heeded the admonition of the Court and have neither listened to radio or television nor read papers concerning the case. I know that this imposes a hardship upon jurors, but the only alternative is to have jurors locked up for the duration of the trial and that is even more of a hardship.

"The jury will remember and heed the admonition of the Court. Gentlemen, you may proceed if you are ready."

"We are ready," Hamilton Burger said.

"We are ready, Your Honor," Mason rejoined.

"Then call your next witness."

Mason said, "Mr. Paul Drake, will you take the stand, please?"

Drake held up his hand, was sworn and took his position on the witness stand.

"What is your occupation?" Mason asked.

"I am a private detective."

"Are you familiar with the Barclay Country Club in this city?"

"I am."

"Are you familiar with the particular portion of the club which is in the vicinity of the seventh tee?"

"Yes, sir."

"When were you last there?"

"Yesterday afternoon at about three to four o'clock."

"What were you doing on the golf course at that hour?"

"I was participating in a search of the territory immediately adjacent to the seventh tee."

"Were you using your eyes or did you have some mechanical assistance?"

"We had a metal detector."

"And did you, at that time, discover anything?"

"Yes, sir."

"What?"

"We discovered a thirty-two-caliber empty, brass cartridge case."

"What did you do with that?"

"You took it into your possession."

Mason approached the witness and said, "I ask you if you made any identifying mark upon that cartridge case?"

"Yes, sir, a small scratch with the point of my knife."

"I show you an empty cartridge case and ask you if that is the cartridge case."

"Yes, sir, that is the one we found."

"If the Court please, we ask this be introduced in evidence as Defendant's Exhibit Number One," Mason said.

Hamilton Burger, on his feet, smiled at the court. "I believe, if the Court please, I have the right to examine the witness on *voir dire*."

"You certainly do," Judge Alvarado said. "Proceed."

"You state that you are a private detective, Mr. Drake?" Hamilton Burger asked, facing the witness.

"Yes, sir."

"You do a great deal of work for Mr. Perry Mason?"

"Yes, sir."

"Does his work account for all of your income?"

"No, sir, not all of it."

"A substantial part of it?"

"Yes, sir."

"As much as ninety per cent?"

"No, I would say perhaps as much as seventy-five per cent."

"I see," Hamilton Burger said. "Now, what are your regular rates of payment?"

"Fifty dollars a day and expenses."

"That is figured on an eight-hour day?"

"Theoretically, yes."

"That is something over six dollars an hour," Hamilton Burger said, "over ten cents a minute. Now, I take it that you are a good businessman and as such you strive to give Mr. Mason value received?"

"We try to keep our clients satisfied. Yes, sir."

"And you try to find what they want?"

"If we can do so, yes."

"You knew when you went out to the golf links that you were going to be searching for an empty cartridge case?"

"I so understood."

"And this cartridge case which you say that you found, there is nothing about it to show when it was fired?"

"No, sir."

"Nor is there anything about it to show when it was dropped on the ground."

"No, sir."

"It could have been dropped on the ground as much as a year ago?"

"I presume so."

"Or it could have been dropped to the ground within a matter of seconds before you so fortuitously found it."

Drake said, "There is nothing about the cartridge case, nor was there anything on the ground telling how long it had been on the ground."

"It could have been a matter of seconds?"

"I presume it *could* have been dropped at any time before we started searching."

"Or it might have been dropped during the search?" Burger asked with a sneer.

"I don't think so."

"You don't *think* so. Can you swear that it hadn't been?"

"I was watching."

"Were you watching every one of the people in your group all the time? Were you watching all of the assembled curiosity seekers who ceased playing golf to cluster around you?"

"It was physically impossible to watch everyone."

"So anyone in that group could have taken advantage of

a time when your back was turned and tossed that empty cartridge case out into the grass?"

"I presume so, yes."

"That empty cartridge case has no commercial value?"

"No."

"But the value of your relationship with Mr. Mason is very great. In other words, his business represents an income of many thousands of dollars a year to you, does it not?"

"It has in the past."

"And you hope it will in the future?"

"Yes, sir."

"As long as you continue to serve him diligently."

"Yes, sir."

"And manage to *find* the articles that he wants you to find."

"I simply work to the best of my ability," Drake said.

"That is all," Hamilton Burger said, as he walked back to the counsel table with a manner that indicated that he was deliberately and contemptuously turning his back on the witness.

Mason, observing the gesture, whispered to Della Street, "The old so-and-so is certainly a past master of courtroom strategy."

"That concludes your *voir dire?*" Judge Alvarado asked Burger.

"Yes, sir."

"The defense has offered this in evidence. Do you have any objection?"

"I certainly do, Your Honor. I object on the ground it is incompetent, irrelevant and immaterial. It is a physical impossibility that this could have been fired from the murder weapon. Therefore, it has no significance standing by itself. The only possible significance could be in the place where it was found, or the time when it was found; and it has just been shown by the evidence of this witness who so fortuitously participated in *finding* this cartridge case, that it is impossible to vouch for the time when it was placed there."

"Nevertheless," Judge Alvarado said, "I think that, while

your objection goes to the weight rather than to the admissibility of the evidence, the Court is going to allow this to be received in evidence. Counsel will have ample opportunity to argue to the jury as to what this means."

"In that case," Hamilton Burger said, "while I realize that this matter should be handled expeditiously, I would like to have a recess until tomorrow morning to try to find out more about this most fortuitous discovery."

Judge Alvarado frowned, started to shake his head.

Mason said, "We have no objections; if the prosecution wants this continuance, the defendant is willing to join in the motion, and since the jurors are not being confined, it should not work too great a hardship upon them."

"Very well," Judge Alvarado said, "on that understanding I will grant the motion, rather reluctantly, however."

Judge Alvarado turned to the jurors. "The jurors will understand that the Court is empowered to keep the jurors together during the trial of a case. This sometimes works an unnecessary hardship; and, if in the judgment of the Court it is not necessary, the Court is permitted to let the jurors return to their homes. The Court will admonish you, however, that the jurors will be violating their oath if they listen to any television discussion of this case, any comment about it on radio, or read anything in the newspapers. The jurors are again admonished not to form or express any opinion in regard to the merits of the case, not to discuss it among yourselves, and not to permit any person to discuss it in your presence.

"Under those circumstances, and in view of the fact that there has been a joint request for a continuance, the Court is somewhat reluctantly taking a recess until tomorrow morning at ten o'clock."

Judge Alvarado left the bench.

Paul Drake, his expression ominous, came over to stand by Mason while he glared across at the prosecution's table.

Hamilton Burger managed to avoid meeting the detective's eyes.

"Take it easy, Paul," Mason warned.

"Someday," Drake said, "I'm going to plant a punch right in the middle of his snout."

"He's only doing his duty," Mason said.

"Well, I don't like the way he does it."

"Neither do I," Mason agreed, "but there are some things about the way I conduct a case which he doesn't like."

"If he'll only look up here," Drake said, "I'll wish him a very good evening in a tone of voice which will be as sarcastic as his voice was when he said, 'That's all.'"

Mason got up, took Drake's arm and gently turned him around. "You'll do nothing of the sort," he said. "That isn't the sort of publicity we want at this particular stage of the game."

"You think the jurors are going to refrain from reading the newspapers?" Drake asked.

Mason smiled. "Come on, Paul, let's both quit being naïve."

Mason picked up his briefcase and smiled at Della Street.

Chapter 23

Back in his office, Della handed Mason the newspapers. "You take a good picture," she said.

"You're the one who takes a good picture," he told her. "Getting that outfit was a stroke of genius on which I pride myself.

"I think," he continued, "that the picture might not have been published if it hadn't been for the feminine angle."

"Angle?" she asked archly.

"Curve," Mason corrected.

She smiled.

Mason read the account in the paper.

"No wonder Hamilton Burger felt peeved," he said. "This makes quite a story."

Mason finished with the paper, started to put it aside; then a headline on an inside page caught his eye.

"Well," he said, "the decedent, Rodger Palmer, seems to have had his name cleared posthumously."

"How come?"

"Another one of those mysterious stocking murders in a cheap hotel.

"You remember that the report made by Drake's detective stated that at one time the police considered Palmer a suspect. He'd lived in two of the hotels where these stocking murders had been committed. He was in the hotel at the time of the crime. . . . That was just a little too much of a coincidence for the police.

"They, of course, took the names of every person residing in the hotel at the time of the crime and then checked those names with the guest lists of other hotels. When they found Palmer's name on two lists, they descended on him like a ton of bricks."

"That certainly was a coincidence," Della Street said.

Mason nodded. "Those things happen in real life, and yet— Hang it, it *is* quite a coincidence. We'd have given it a lot of thought if it hadn't been that Palmer was very dead by the time we started investigating him.

"Get me that report from Drake's operative, Della. Let's study it again."

Della Street went to the file, returned with a report on the dead man.

Mason thumbed through the numerous typewritten sheets of flimsy. "The guy seems to have been pretty much of a lone wolf," he said, "never married, an oil worker, then down and out—sort of a sharpshooter.

"He may have been a professional blackmailer. He had something on the Steer Ridge Oil and Refining Company that was worth money to someone, or at least he thought it was. He was fighting for proxies . . . and he must have had something rather degrading on Fred Hedley—probably a prior marriage that had never been dissolved."

Mason slowly thumbed through the pages of the report; then went back and reread it.

Abruptly the lawyer straightened himself in the office chair, started to say something, checked himself, looked up at Della and back to the report.

"Something?" she asked.

"I don't know," Mason said thoughtfully.

The lawyer got up and started pacing the floor. Della, knowing his habits, sat very quietly so she would not interrupt his thinking. Later on, when the lawyer had clarified the situation in his own mind, she might ask him questions so that by answering those questions he could crystallize his thoughts, but right at the moment she knew he needed an opportunity for complete concentration.

Mason suddenly paused in his pacing.

"Della," he said, "I want an ad in the papers that will be in the night editions."

As she started to say something, Mason said, "I know that's impossible. I know those want ad pages are printed in advance, but I want this in a box somewhere in the newspapers, entitled, 'Too Late To Classify,' or something of that sort. Tell them that it's important to get it in. Money's no object."

"What's the copy?" she asked.

"Make it this way. Put the initials, capital P, capital M; then, 'The thing that was too hot for the grass on the golf course is now even more valuable than ever. Call this number at nine o'clock sharp and follow instructions.' "

"And the number?" Della Street asked.

Mason said, "Go to a service station in Hollywood. Find a telephone booth; get the number.

"Now then, you're going to have to work fast. You're going to have to get co-operation from the papers. Tell them it's a red-hot tip and if they'll put the ad in and say nothing about it to anyone, they may get a red-hot story later on.

"Then, while you're pulling wires, I'll get Paul Drake and we'll get an operative we can trust who will be at this number at exactly nine o'clock with instructions to act as decoy in case somebody bites on our little scheme."

"And in case no one bites?" Della Street asked.

"Then," Mason said, "Burger can show that Paul Drake got another fifty-dollar charge on his bill."

Della Street typed out the want ad, said, "I'm on my way."

Mason called Paul Drake. "Paul," he said, "I want an operative to be at a public pay station at nine o'clock sharp tonight, and if he is contacted there, to make an appointment to meet whoever calls at one of the most lonely, secluded spots your man will be able to pick out during the afternoon.

"That spot has to be wooded. It has to be within a reasonable distance of the highway. It has to be unlighted."

"Have a heart, Perry," Drake said. "About the only place I know of would be a golf course, and we've had enough of golf courses in this case."

"Golf courses are out," Mason said. "Try a city dump."

"Suppose no one calls the operative when he's in the service station?"

"Then," Mason said, "we'll give him a call and give him further instructions.

"Get busy, Paul. This is of real importance. It may be the payoff."

"You have a live lead?" Drake asked.

"I'm playing a hunch," Mason said. "It's a wild hunch, but it may pay off."

Mason hung up; then picked up the other telephone and said to Gertie at the switchboard, "Get me Homicide at the police department, Gertie. I want to talk to Lieutenant Tragg."

"No one else, if he's out?"

"If he's out," Mason said, "I don't even want anyone to know who's calling."

Chapter 24

Perry Mason, Lt. Tragg, Della Street, Paul Drake and one of Drake's operatives huddled in the dark shadows of a group of stunted trees.

In their nostrils was the sour smell of a city dump.

"You certainly picked a sweet-smelling place," Lt. Tragg said.

Drake, speaking in a hushed voice, said, "It was the only one that we could find that gave us what we wanted."

Tragg said, "Now, let's have this definitely understood. There's to be no publicity."

"No publicity unless *you* give it publicity," Mason said.

"I don't publicize my wild goose chases," Tragg said. "I don't want the D.A.'s office to know anything about this, and I'm risking my official neck just trying to play ball with you."

"I've put the cards on the table," Mason said.

"You certainly did, and I never saw such a collection of jokers in my life," Tragg grunted.

Paul Drake nervously reached for a cigarette, then checked himself as he remembered the admonition of no smoking.

Night insects shrilled in the distance. Somewhere a chorus of frogs started croaking, then lapsed into silence, then started croaking again.

"Suppose no one calls him?" Tragg asked.

"At five minutes past nine," Mason said, "one of Drake's operatives will call him. The phone will ring and the man in the booth will pick up the receiver just as though it were a bona fide call."

"And then?" Tragg asked.

"Then he'll start for here."

"And if anyone calls?"

"We'll know we're on the right track," Mason said.

"Well," Tragg told him, "that's the trouble with amateurs. You get crazy ideas. I'll bet ten to one no one calls him."

"We'll know pretty quick," Mason said, consulting his wrist watch and then raising the antenna on a walkie-talkie.

"He isn't carrying a walkie-talkie with him, is he?" Tragg asked.

"No," Mason said. "But he does have a citizen's band transceiver on his car, but I wanted to use a walkie-talkie for receiving because we don't want to have any loud noises."

Suddenly the walkie-talkie in the hands of Perry Mason made squawking noises, then a little pinched voice said, "Do you read me?"

"I read you. Come in," Mason said. "What's happened?"

"I'm on my way out."

"Call?"

"Only the decoy one we'd arranged."

"Okay," Mason said, his voice showing disappointment, "we'll follow plan number two. Over and off."

The lawyer snapped down the antenna on the walkie-talkie.

"Well," he said dejectedly, "it looks as if you win, Lieutenant."

Tragg snorted. "I would have bet you a hundred to one—a thousand to one."

"Well," Mason said, "the only chance now is that someone was watching and will follow him in a car."

"That's a good ten-thousand-to-one bet," Tragg said. "I'm holding you to your promise, Mason, that you'll never betray me on this."

"You have my word," Mason told him. "Come on, let's deploy out into the shadows near the road. Drake's man is instructed to get out of the car and walk directly toward the dump for thirty-five paces, then stop, stand in the open for a few seconds, and then move into the shadows and drop to the ground."

Tragg said, "All right, we've stuck our necks out this far. Now we'll play along with your plan number two."

They moved slowly according to prearranged plan into the dense shadows near the roadway.

"How long will it take him to get here?" Tragg asked.

"We figured twelve minutes on a trial run this afternoon," Mason said.

"All right," Tragg said, "I've held the bag on your snipe hunting this far and I may as well throw twelve minutes down the rathole."

They waited until headlights appeared on the dirt road—headlights which danced up and down over the bumpy road, at times sending a beam up into the trees, at times pointing down as the car negotiated the bumps.

"That road is full of nails and tire hazards," Drake said. "I'll bet we have tire trouble with one of these cars."

"Don't be so pessimistic," Mason said. "Lieutenant Tragg has infected you with the gloom bug."

The car came to a stop. The headlights were switched off. A dark figure jumped from the car, walked rapidly for thirty-five steps, then stood for approximately thirty seconds, then moved into the shadows and dropped to the ground.

"Well," Tragg said, "the show's over. We may as well call it a night and go home."

"Wait a minute," Mason said. "We've got to give our quarry a chance."

"Your quarry!" Lt. Tragg snorted sarcastically.

"Silence!" Mason warned. "I think I heard the motor of a car."

They remained silent.

Drake said in a harsh whisper, "You're right. A car without headlights!"

The little group remained tense as the sound of a motor became plainly audible, a motor in a car which was being driven without headlights.

Abruptly the car came to a stop.

"If *this* thing works," Tragg muttered, "I'll be a monkey's uncle." And then after a moment, he added ruefully,

"And if it doesn't work and this ever gets out, I'll be the monkey himself."

"Hush!" Mason whispered.

They held their positions, listening and watching. The dark shadows played tricks on their eyes. Once Della Street grasped Mason's arm, said, "Something moved."

No one else, however, had seen the movement.

They waited five minutes. Tragg sucked in his breath, starting to say something when, suddenly, they all saw a figure silhouetted against a patch of night sky.

Mason pressed the button of the powerful flashlight he was holding.

A figure interfused a forearm between eyes and flashlight. There was a glint of metal on blued-steel, then an orange spreading flash and the whistle of a bullet going past Mason's head.

The lawyer extinguished the flashlight. "Come on!" he said.

The group ran forward.

Twice more the reddish orange flame spurted into the night. Twice more they heard the whistle of bullets, then there were no more shots.

"We use plan three!" Mason shouted. "We don't want to kill unless we have to, and we don't want to move in and be sitting ducks."

They froze into immobility for what seemed an interminable period of silence, then, suddenly, they heard the roar of a car motor as it throbbed into life, and a second later headlights came on. The car, a hundred yards down the road, tried to make a U-turn, stalled, backed, crashed into a tree, then started forward.

The group ran to Lt. Tragg's police car which had been hidden in the brush. They climbed in hurriedly. Tragg throbbed the motor into life, switched on the red light, hit the siren, and at the same time called in on the radio asking the dispatcher to head off a car which was proceeding at high speed from the dirt road into the dump, asking that roadblocks be put up on the principal paved roads leading from the dirt road.

The car had traveled wildly, the taillights glowing like red rubies.

Tragg, driving the car with police competency, hustled over the road, gaining on the car ahead.

Abruptly the lights on the other car were switched off.

"Trying to find a side road to turn down," Tragg grunted, and switched on a powerful searchlight.

The searchlight not only held the car ahead in the beam of its illumination but the reflection in the windshield blinded the driver.

Again the lights of the car ahead were switched on, but during the period of dark driving the car had lost valuable ground.

The fleeing car made a screaming turn from the dirt road onto the pavement, and suddenly the blood-red brake lights flared into brilliance as the driver frantically depressed the brake pedal.

A police car was parked broadside in the road, and on each side of the police car were officers with drawn guns.

"I guess that does it," Tragg said.

"Let's hope she doesn't have enough presence of mind to throw the gun away," Mason said. "That's our best evidence."

The fugitive's car skidded to a stop. Mrs. Hedley's hate-distorted features were illuminated by the glaring lights as she slowly got out of her car with her hands up.

Tragg stopped his car immediately behind hers, and the party piled out.

Mrs. Hedley looked at them with venomous hatred.

Her eyes came to focus on Perry Mason's face. "How I wish I could have killed you!" she spat at him.

Tragg pushed past her, looked in the automobile and picked up an automatic from the seat.

"This is your gun?" he asked.

"See my lawyer," she snapped.

"You won't need to ask any questions," Mason said. "Take that gun to ballistics. Check the empty cartridge case we found at the seventh tee for what the ballistics experts call the breech-block signature and you'll find the cartridge was fired from that gun."

Another car came driving up behind. Drake's operative got out and said, "Gosh, you folks get a man into all sorts of scrapes."

Perry Mason grinned at him. "When you get on the stand," he said, "tell Hamilton Burger that you were collecting the regular fee of fifty dollars a day and that you were shot at three times—all of which is only part of the day's work."

Chapter 25

Paul Drake, Della Street and Kerry Dutton were gathered in Mason's office the next afternoon. Dutton, still somewhat dazed from the rapid developments of the day, said, "Would you mind telling me how you did all this?"

Mason grinned. "I didn't," he said. "Lieutenant Tragg did. Lieutenant Tragg had to."

"Well, the papers certainly gave Tragg a wonderful spread of publicity. One would have thought he originated the whole idea."

"An officer has to take credit," Mason said. "It's part of the game. When Tragg consented to go with me, he knew I'd give him all the publicity if the scheme paid off—and keep him out of it if it didn't."

"But how did you know what had happened?"

"It was just simple reasoning," Mason said. "So simple that I almost overlooked it.

"Palmer was killed shortly after nine o'clock, but the murderess needed a Patsy, so the murderess picked on you. She decoyed you into going to the scene of the murder because she knew Palmer had been trying to put the bite on you. Just before you arrived, the murderess fired another shot so that if anyone happened to be listening, there would be the sound of a shot that would coincide with the time the murder was supposed to have taken place.

"Then, of course, you very stupidly played into the hands of the murderess just as she had expected you would, because she had planted Desere's gun by the body—a gun which she had taken from the bureau drawer in Desere's bedroom."

"And the reason?" Drake asked.

"Not the reason that any of us had thought of.

"Palmer had been in two hotels when these stocking strangulation murders had taken place. The police had, quite naturally, considered him as a suspect, but very foolishly they didn't consider him as a witness. They didn't ask him in detail about the people he had seen in the hotel although he probably wouldn't have told them if they had asked.

"We know now that he had seen Hedley in each of the hotels, and Hedley was the mysterious person who had registered under an assumed name and then vanished. The description fits him."

"And Mrs. Hedley knew what her son had done?"

"Her son has been a little bit off ever since he was a boy. She has a fierce protective instinct—an instinct which was strong enough to make her willing to kill if she had to in order to protect her boy.

"But the point is Palmer knew what Hedley had done, and Palmer desperately needed money to win his proxy fight in the Steer Ridge Oil Company. He felt that he could ultimately gain a million if he could only get operating capital.

"So Palmer put the bite on Mrs. Hedley. It was blackmail for the highest stakes possible. Either he got money or he put the police on the trail of her son on a series of murders.

"That's always a dangerous gambit. Palmer knew that, but he was playing for big stakes. He had to take the chance.

"And he lost his gamble."

"Hedley, himself, didn't—"

"Hedley, himself, didn't know anything about Palmer's murder," Mason went on. "It was his mother who was trying to protect him; his mother who killed the man who could have betrayed her son.

"When you stop to think of it, it had to be the mother. She could have had access to the bureau drawer in Desere's apartment. She was the only one who could have secured that gun, who had a sufficiently strong motive to commit murder if she had to.

"Hedley really gave himself away during that fight with

you, Kerry. He ran into Desere's bedroom. He was looking for a nylon stocking. If he'd got his hands on one you'd have found him an expert garroter. He's had lots of practice.

"It was thinking about that rush to the bedroom and trying to find the reason for it that started me thinking along the right line."

Dutton shook his head. "I can still feel the arms of that metallic chair in the gas chamber."

"You certainly led with your chin," Mason told him, "trying to protect the girl you loved and trying to surprise her with an inheritance.

"Now then, make me a check for five thousand dollars covering my fee and Drake's expenses. Get out of here, hunt up Desere Ellis, tell her you love her and ask her to marry you."

"That last," Dutton said, "is probably the best advice I've *ever* had."